THE WE AND THE THEY

THE WE
AND
THE THEY

KYRA ANN DAWKINS

NEW DEGREE PRESS

COPYRIGHT © 2020 KYRA ANN DAWKINS

THE WE AND THE THEY

ISBN   978-1-64137-952-6 *Paperback*
           978-1-64137-766-9 *Kindle Ebook*
           978-1-64137-768-3 *Ebook*

CONTENTS

A NOTE FROM THE AUTHOR

As I write this, I can't help but imagine you tracing these words in your mind. Everything about this seems normal until these traced words become a path you follow to my smooth and warm mahogany writing desk. Actually, I don't have a physical writing desk. It is more of a symbolic mental space I carve out for myself in steal-away moments of the day. And yet, here you are, standing next to me by my desk.

Reasonably bewildered, your wide eyes ask me, "How did I get here?"

Good question. I'll answer that in a moment.

As I suppress my initial impulse to give you an awkward military handshake, I meet your gaze and coolly say, "Welcome, reader. Would you like to have a seat?"

You nod, and a plush, golden velvet armchair materializes next to you. You sit down. We're going to be here for a while, so we might as well make ourselves comfortable.

Now that you're all settled in, on to answering your question. How did you get here? Well, you were summoned here by the nature of this story. Each story calls for a certain kind of audience, and this one has insisted on you. Simple. Admittedly strange, but still simple. I can see you're uneasy. Probably still a tad winded from the trip here. I validate your feelings and concerns. A lot of this is new to me, too. But it will make more sense as we go along. There is no need to worry.

Trust me.

As you may have noticed on your way in, this particular story is called *The We and the They*. In all honesty, I know just as much as you do in terms of what this story is *about*. We will find that out together later on. But since I have been here just a bit longer than you have, I *can* tell you what this story *does*. Maybe that will help.

In *The We and the They*, the voices ebb and flow out of one collective voice. This story seeks to honor the significance of oral history in the formation of collective identities. My grandfather told me stories like this one. Hearing stories that I know have been passed down for generations in my family is captivating. Many of my favorite childhood memories are of my grandfather, after making sure each of his grandkids were ready for bed, acting out his favorite stories in his soft, yet bellowing baritone voice. Some of the stories were fairy tales or old wives' tales, some were performed as folk songs, and others were oral histories of our family's survival. Though I think these stories would have still been important to me if they were written down in a book, my grandfather made the stories come alive with his distinct voice. His stories helped me develop an understanding of myself outside of societally-encouraged individuality. My grandfather inspired me to become a story dweller. Listening to and cherishing the stories he told became even more important to me as I got older and realized how much my ancestors endured to ensure these stories would reach my ears.

Stories can chronicle and propel survival through suffering long before they are ever written down. They can help people navigate the balance between memory and movement in constructing their own sense of self. Even the words of some of the most sacred texts, like the Bible, were on the minds, hearts, and lips of believers before they were etched on scrolls. The narratives in the Bible and the ones passed down through my family would not have been able to shape who I am without the resilience of oral tradition.

The We and the They, guided by oral tradition, points to parts of a whole. It carries stones toward building foundations of legacy. This story calls us to remember the importance of sharing with one another and processing emotions in community. We live in an "I" world. That can be unsettling at times. Each of us, in some capacity or another, is expected to curate our own "I," whether it be through sharpened words on résumés, perfected profile pictures, or optimized career networks. We are told to brand ourselves with the "I" at the center of storming societal demands. And we are expected to do all of this with heart-racing efficiency, with barely enough time to breath or orient ourselves to changing environments.

Please do not misunderstand. The "I" is not bad or intrinsically problematic or evil. Far from it. The "I" can be useful, even beneficial. It helps each of us articulate our own needs and hopes. It prevents us from putting words that don't belong in one another's mouths. The "I" gives a voice to the individual parts of ourselves, which is crucial to formulating our unique identities. But any "I" can only be healthy and helpful if it is rooted in the rich mixed soils of "We."

When I dwell in this story, I can more easily acknowledge that my "I" is part of greater "Wes." I, as an individual, can only begin to make sense of myself in terms of collectives. But this story is trying to create new "Wes." That is why you are here. You and I, fellow story dwellers, are a "We" now because of this story. Do you see what I mean?

I can tell you're still nervous. It's okay. So am I. There really is no need to worry, though. Trust me. I am right here with you.

We are right here for each other.

PROLOGUE

We owe it to ourselves to start with some sort of beginning. Our collective genesis guides our heartbeat as We run. We can feel a shared, blood-rushing pulse in our temples. And all of us, even in the time before, believed in a version of the same proverb: the future is only born through honoring the past. We owe this knowledge to our children. We must hold this knowledge in our strides. Muscle memory. Otherwise, our children, for generations to come, will have a piercing hunger for a sense of origin. That kind of hunger knows no boundaries. When it has had enough of carving pits in stomachs, it starts gnawing away at sinews, gorging on flesh, worming through minds. We are all too familiar with its greedy pain. Never again. But this hunger and our vow against it made us who We are.

We were not always We.

In the time before the Great Famine, We were scattered across our respective lands, milling and seeding, droning and slicing. Mountains, oceans, and warring interests divided us. We vied for the right to have more than the others, entitled to opulence. We despised one another and the earth became weary of being caught in the crossfire. If We were honest with ourselves back then, We might have acknowledged the earth's anger after millennia upon millennia of stealing her fruits to fuel our hatred. Now, We often tell each other the Great Famine was the earth's defeated sigh in the wake of our foolishness. All of us, in our respective lands, had once gotten everything We needed from the earth. But with the start of the Great Famine, our stomachs were hollowed with a new kind of emptiness.

The whole world became a wilderness. Oases shriveled away, poisoned by the merciless ground. Some of us who were from deserts watched in horror as red clay soil cracked in anguish, overbaked in the sun's heat. Others of us who voyaged through seas mourned martyred fish, fevered waters, and ocean-swallowed islands. Those of us who dwelled in forests knew the trees were petrified by suffering too, unable to blossom or bear fruit. And even the ones among us who once lived in nature-suppressed cities experienced climatic loss, shifting tectonic plates, flooding streets, ripping wind, crumbling foundations. Nothing was stable—the weather rebellious, everything scorched or frozen or slashed or drenched. We all had no choice but to wander away from the homes that had once been so kind to us. Sojourners with no known destination, We heaved for breath while chasing mirages.

We often disagree among ourselves about how exactly We came together. Even fairly recent events are obscured by diverse and questionable memories. When basic survival is at stake, exact chronology tends to not be a primary concern. Fortunately, consensus isn't always necessary for a shared story.

How long did We wander through the world during the Great Famine? We have too many ways to keep and frame time to answer that precisely or honestly. We could try to reach back and make vain attempts to measure that miserable slice of infinity. Perhaps, we measure by the number of times the moon waxed and waned, or by how many once-bleeding cuts crusted over and flaked away, or by how sparingly We allowed ourselves to indulge in laughter. Suffice to say, We were in the wilderness for longer than anyone would care or imagine to be.

How did We learn to understand one another? We complicated this issue for the better. Even before the Great Famine emerged, in order to be deemed a person of worth in the world, one had to speak Common Tongue. Some of us only knew Common Tongue. Most of us spoke it and our native languages. And a few of us had only heard it a couple of times before. Perhaps it would have been easier to resort to solely communicating in Common Tongue. That's probably what We did in our earliest days as a group. But Common Tongue carried a dark history and many of us missed the familiar words of our homelands. So, to distract ourselves from hunger, We challenged one another to read facial expressions and gestures. We used our fingers to draw pictures in the dirt or sand. We exchanged phrases until We could gather enough shards of each other's languages to form the mosaic of an operating new one. This language is *ours* now but We still don't agree on what to call it.

How did We grow as a group? Whenever We encountered people wandering, We offered them the chance to join us if they were willing to abide by our terms of sharing the little We had. Some were willing, some were not. Those who were became part of us. Simple. The simplest part of all of it, really.

Why? Why what? *Why did We decide to become We?*

We want to believe it was out of regard for human dignity. Sometimes, We like to say We were too humble to choose who had the right to have and those who didn't. And perhaps those things were somewhat true. But in reality, We were too exhausted to kill each other. It was impossible to plot murder when parched tongues clung to the roofs of needy mouths. Besides, hunger was our enemy. Why would We have wasted our energy warring against one another? It was an oxymoronic, yet altruistic common sense that worked by some miracle. None of us ate until We were satisfied but We had enough for all of us to subsist. Our collective survival depended on each other.

Yet in time, We grew weary of having stomach groans as lullabies. That was why We were so willing to believe them.

They seemed to be an answer to our prayers. They were beautiful at first. Their strides were long and assured as They neared us. It was as if They already knew who We were. Their skin glistened in a way that was more than human. Mystic. Angelic. Metallic. Golden. God-sent. Gorgeous. These were no ordinary wanderers. But most startlingly, once They only were a breath away, They kneeled before us in reverence.

"Come with us," They insisted in Common Tongue, their voices bellowing. "We have found an oasis. A group of us have settled there and started a farm. There is plenty of food. More than milk and honey. If you join us, we will provide a great feast in celebration and many more to come. You all are welcome to eat from our table."

By then, a type of desperation that superseded suspicion had seized us all. Hunger was our enemy, after all, and They would slay it. We went with them. And it is difficult to tell whether that was the end of our beginnings or the beginning of their ends.

* * *

Now, We are running from the very ones who promised to feed us. The night dew that once quenched our thirst mingles with blood from our blistered feet. But We are like wild horses carried by the wind, galloping too fast to feel the sting. We aren't afraid of the darkness. We welcome it as an old, forgotten friend. We prefer darkness over the hollowing lantern light or greedy furnace flame.

To be clear, They did not lie to us. They did in fact feed us. We ate at their ornate and abundant table of delectable absurdities. Oftentimes, We couldn't recognize what We were told to consume. Yet, even in the time before the Great Famine, We all believed some version of another proverb: don't bite the hand that feeds you. It could have been worse. We could have been an army of Ezekiel's walking skeletons. But We aren't. Not anymore. We would always eat until We were more than full as They watched us with their steel-bullet eyes.

"Let nothing go to waste," They'd bark, as They would refuse to untie our legs from the chairs until We finished every morsel on our plates. The thick, weathered rope would burn and chafe our skin. "Let nothing go to waste," They'd growl. "Let nothing go to waste." We are sure that demons will tell them the same thing when They are forced to politely gnaw on their own flesh at a banquet table in hell. That is, of course, if any kind of divine justice exists in this life or the next. We believe there is. God has kept most of us alive thus far. We've lost Adelaide, Rose, Samson, Zenith, Jordan, and Isaac. While We were all held in a mirage amid famished scarcity, each of them died from things they swallowed. We hope to find a place where We can properly mourn for them, our beloved own. They are still with us as We run.

We are heading to the last place where We were all together before They tricked us. A hallowed place where the moon bathes in the river by a frail, solemn willow tree. And tonight, it won't only be the moon that dares to wade through those putrid waters. We are far enough away from their farm-centered oasis to see the crippling effects of the Great Famine again. Everything in this river is dead, except for the moon, insidious unseen creatures, and of course, the leeches.

ADELAIDE

Leeches. Those disgustingly gluttonous creatures with their greedy, salivating mouths. Lord knows why they even exist. But Adelaide used to always insist We should love the vile things, since leeches are part of God's creation, too. Adelaide was strangely sentimental when it came to animals. We can still see her sitting near the riverbank, waiting for the leeches to finish feasting on her arms and legs, until they, with their bulging stomachs, softly fell and she could lay them back in the water. The rest of us, the sensible ones, took turns using the smoldering end of a stick from the young fire We'd built to burn the leeches until they dropped in defeat as gnarled black shells.

Adelaide was too precocious then to look at us with horror. She understood our fear but she was still sad as she gently rebuked us. "We should not be the ones causing unnatural death. Death itself wasn't meant to be natural before the Fall."

The faithful willow reminds us of her.

* * *

"Excuse me. Have any of you seen a gray squirrel with a black streak in her tail? She's one of a kind around here and I need to make sure she's safe."

Quite a while before We encountered the inhumane ones, Adelaide found us on the outer rim of the vast, dying forest she called home. She almost looked as if she were made from the woods. Her skin was warm, tree-bark brown, and covered in scrapes, and her eyes were green with the rusted tinge of aging leaves. Adelaide was notably tall with gangly limbs, skin-and-bones thin from the famine. And her long, coiling hair was filled with small twigs. We weren't sure how old she was, and We later discovered that neither was she. She was no longer a child but she also wasn't quite a woman. Her nimble movements and trusting gaze made it clear she was young.

We were taken aback by her boldness and, at first, stunned into silence.

"Please," Adelaide firmly pleaded. "The squirrel's name is Muriel, and I'm fairly certain she is pregnant. I would really appreciate your help in finding her."

Rose, the one among us who was probably closest to Adelaide's age, spoke first. "Have you tried calling the squirrel's name? Muriel, I mean?"

"I have, but I think she may be out of earshot. She moves a lot faster than you might think, pregnant and all. But she usually doesn't wander this far away from her nest. Will you help me look for her?"

We all pitied Adelaide then, especially Rose. This was partly because she was so *desperate* to find a squirrel, but mostly because she was so desperate to find a *squirrel*. Perhaps hunger and loneliness had made her go mad.

"Sure," said Rose. "I'll help you look for Muriel. We both just have to be back here with the rest of the group before dark."

It was a subtle invitation but Adelaide was quick to notice it. People tend to connect most in the space beyond words. So much can emerge from confident intonation. Understanding that more than the rest of us, Rose wanted to claim Adelaide as our own through an exchange of weighted glances.

With a slight nod, Adelaide responded, "Okay. We'll be back here before dark."

As it turned out, after trekking through the forest for most of the afternoon, Adelaide and Rose found Muriel in her home nest at twilight, nursing the three babies she had just birthed. Adelaide was disappointed that she had missed the births.

"New life is beautiful in times like these, you know? Thank God Muriel and her babies seem healthy and fine. I wish I could have been there for her though. Just this one last time."

That night, We explained the official terms for Adelaide to join us. She needed to be willing to share like the rest of us, striving against hunger but still prioritizing community. Adelaide readily agreed. And for good measure, some of us added more conditions.

"For one thing," Rose began, "so help me, but you are going to need to let me get those gnarled twigs and tangles out of your hair. I'll even carve the comb myself."

Adelaide laughed in a wind-rustling-through-trees way. Then, Rose laughed, and soon We were all laughing, from light chuckles to hearty guffaws. None of us had laughed like that for a long time.

Adelaide was almost always exuberant, radiating a vibrant and persistent joy. But We knew tragedy had deeply marked her young life. Whenever We tried to ask Adelaide about her past and family, she would describe her daily life taking care of the animals, who she saw as siblings. She knew her parents had died just as she had finished learning to speak her native language and Common Tongue. She knew they died in some unnatural way but her mind suppressed the memories of losing them.

Adelaide could not remember how long it had been just her and the forest creatures before We came. She was able to subsist on the little food and water the forest still provided.

Adelaide also had a deep knowledge of medicinal plants, grinding mosses and herbs to make salves for wounds.

"God gives us everything We need in nature," Adelaide would say, rubbing green paste on an open sore. "We just need to know how to respect his creation. How to be kind to it."

We made jars out of hardened mud and old leaves to carry Adelaide's remedies with us as We journeyed beyond the woods. We had just run out of the ointments by the time They found us.

* * *

After They deceived us, Adelaide was delighted to discover We'd be staying on the largest farm any of us had ever seen. Acres and acres of plush greenery. Fields and fields of burgeoning produce. Stables and stables of horses. The creatures Adelaide had never seen before but instantly loved.

"My goodness," she gasped, her evergreen eyes wide with wonder. "They're so majestic."

It soon became clear to us that They did not see these seemingly opulent quantities of land and livestock as superfluous or excessive. The expanding size of their enterprise was merely a consequence of its success, and We were the next phase of this expansion. None of us minded then. All of us wanted food by whatever means necessary, and sweet Adelaide just wanted to work with the horses.

Adelaide got her chance. After We arrived, They saw how gentle she was with all the livestock and must have noted her natural affinity for the horses. They positioned her as third-in-command over all the stables, a lofty title that really only amounted to being in charge of shoveling horse dung and polishing the golden carriages They hardly ever used. But Adelaide loved every minute of it. In the evenings, as We were all washing up in preparation for dinner in their big house, Adelaide—in her steady and quickfire way—would tell us all about her day, describing how each of the horses she'd seen were doing with a level of detail only a carefully trained eye could see. She liked all the horses but Adelaide became the fondest of an old mare named April.

"I like April's name," she'd say, "because I think I might've been born sometime during that month. Something brightens in me at the beginning of spring. And I like the way she moves along, all slow and steady-like and persistent. She has a matriarchal air about her, and her spirit reminds me of Muriel."

In the afternoons, Adelaide would ride April to lead all the other horses to the grazing pastures. After April had her fill of lush grass, Adelaide would have her saunter around to watch over the big farm's young foals. Lennox, who Adelaide guessed was April's grandson, was particularly absent-minded and gullible. The poor thing would always get in some kind of trouble. Adelaide could tell April was protective of him.

So, when Lennox strayed beyond the grazing grounds toward the woods yet again, Adelaide was not surprised. But this time, when April galloped over to the border, Adelaide saw something shifting amid the trees. Lennox was gingerly trotting toward the movement as if he were being beckoned. Adelaide felt April tense up. She only did that when an unfamiliar creature came around.

"Excuse me," Adelaide sharply called into the woods in Common Tongue. "What do you think you're doing?"

A tall, faceless figure in a dark cloak materialized from the trees' shadows. "This does not concern you, fleshed one of the forest," the being hissed in Adelaide's native language. "These are sacred matters."

Before Adelaide could stop her, a suddenly enraged April charged toward the cloaked figure.

"And then April and I just passed *through* it, and the figure disintegrated," an astonished Adelaide explained to us later that evening. "It was like moving through smoke."

We assumed that she had just spent too much time working in the hot sun. That Adelaide would come to her senses once she got some sleep. Who could believe a living being could be born from shadows?

* * *

A couple days later, as the dew was still settling after dawn, Adelaide heard them mumbling about how They were going to shoot April the following evening after their visitors left.

"They said April is just a waste of resources," Adelaide told us with righteous anger. "They said she's just a lazy body taking up resources and space. They said she 'disrespected the Embers,' whatever that means. Who cares? April's a valuable living being."

"Adelaide," Rose said consolingly, resting a gentle hand on Adelaide's shoulder, "all They seem to care about here is efficiency. You know that. You see how hard They make us all work. And as painful as it is to acknowledge, April is not an efficient creature. She is a hurdle in their crazed ambitions."

"So what? Yes, April is old and slow most of the time, but she isn't harming anyone around here, and she's so close to living to a full natural life. They should just leave her be. They can't possibly kill her if They have souls."

But Adelaide wasn't going to leave that up to chance.

The afternoon before April's scheduled execution, one of their wives had Adelaide go into another room to fetch much-needed needlepoint supplies. As she recounted the story later that night in a vain effort to lighten the mood, Adelaide performed her best upturned nose and pinched-face impression of the mistress who sent her.

"You. Yes, you, girl. Go and bring me my artistic materials. Be sure those clumsy hands of yours don't drop anything."

While rummaging through the drawers, Adelaide stumbled upon the long, slim key to the arsenal. It was strangely beautiful, with its metal shining a vivid violet.

"And I don't know what came over me," Adelaide explained as she clutched her stomach, her eyes glassy with embryonic tears, "I just swallowed the key."

She just swallowed the key. She *just* swallowed the key?

She could have resisted in other ways. We, as the sensible ones, could have rebuked her and said she could have done so many other things that wouldn't have put her life in jeopardy. She could have hidden the key in her skirt pocket and buried it in the dirtiest part of the farm where They never go. She could have thrown the key to the back of the fireplace or into the furnace. She could have simply put the key in another room, since They think looking for items that are not in their proper place is a waste of their precious energy. But no, she swallowed the key so her righteous and naive act of sacrifice could be closest to her body and heart. And We didn't chastise Adelaide because that would have been a waste of our energy. Instead, when They weren't watching us, We wept over the inevitable.

Adelaide's condition deteriorated quickly. For two weeks after swallowing the key, We watched her spiral into an unnerving oblivion, retching, writhing, and trembling as though some cold, invisible hand twisted her like a rag to wring out the contents of her stomach. Adelaide longed for the medicinal plants of her home forest. They might not have been able to change Adelaide's fate but she remembered a special blend that would have helped ease her pain. But the big farm was far from her home forest, having everything except what she needed, as far as Adelaide knew.

And We couldn't tell them why Adelaide was so sick. Something in us knew that if They found out she had swallowed the arsenal key, she would have received the bullet meant for April. They had little tolerance for defiance. So, We kept quiet about it except for the choked, tearful nights. Rose tried to swallow her sobs but still cried rivers of silent tears as she watched Adelaide fade away. In her grief, Rose would tremble so much that Samson had to wrap his arms around her to keep her from falling. We noticed when They gave up on tying Adelaide to her chair at the table or making sure she was there at all. They must have seen her as a waste of resources.

Their faces and voices stone cold and nonchalant, They told us They found her limp body by the stables next to a pool of vomit and blood. We weren't sure where They took her body. Some of us had hoped to bury her. Others of us had hoped she'd be cremated. All of us felt Adelaide deserved a proper funeral. But They didn't seem to care about acknowledging or honoring the dead. They continued on as if nothing had happened.

Adelaide died an unnatural death, just like her parents, so April and the other aging livestock wouldn't have to. But

They, the soulless ones, forged a new arsenal key and shot April anyway. No one is quite sure what happened to Lennox, either.

* * *

We've just finished wading through the river. As a homage to Adelaide, We are reluctantly waiting for these repulsive leeches to have their fill of our warm blood before they fall off of us in satisfaction and We can place them back in the water. We are doing all We can to keep ourselves from recoiling in horror. Rose would have been the only one who could do this impromptu ceremony with the grace and gravitas it deserves. Rose was the only one who ever really understood Adelaide's strange and selfless love for animals. Rose was the one who understood Adelaide most. But They stole Rose away from us, too.

WE

Hindsight is the clearest and sharpest type of understanding. We know this all too well. We'd like to tell ourselves that if We were in our right minds, We would have left them soon after We'd met them in the desert. We were desperate and naive then. When our clouded minds and famished stomachs were promised food, our stomachs took eager charge over our collective consciousness. In those times, reason would have impeded basic survival.

In all honesty, They charmed us. We were naturally intrigued by their assured demeanor and abundant confidence. And, when They first found us, They mustered their best possible impression of human kindness. Their invitation to join them appeared to be heartfelt and genuine. They dressed our wounds with what felt like silk. Early on in our three-dawn journey toward the big farm, They walked among us, eavesdropping on our conversations in a way We assumed was child-like, almost endearing. Back then, We even did them the favor of speaking Common Tongue instead of our shared constructed language so They could understand us.

But it didn't take long for their façade of warmth to fracture. Soon after the second dawn of our voyage, They stopped walking among us. Instead, some of them marched ahead and some behind us. This must have been to ensure that none of us, their acquired fleshed ones, got lost. But at the time, We felt firmly protected as We followed their directions. We were excited to visit their paradise home as guests. We were so excited, in fact, that We blissfully overlooked the first sign of their cruelty.

It was the second dusk of the farm-bound journey. Most of us were gathering kindling to make fires and insects to roast over the flames. Though They were no longer marching, They were far from idle. Dusk seemed to them as much of a call to action as dawn. They appeared to share that in common with us. Some of us, and most of them, saw dusk as the optimal time for hunting.

In the time before the Great Famine, all of us had come from different cultures with different customs pertaining to hunting animals. Some of us, including Adelaide, could not bring ourselves to eat any kind of meat despite our unrelenting hunger. Others, like Rose and Zenith, ate meat sparingly so that those who preferred meat could have larger rationed portions. And a few of us, including Samson and Jordan, were more carnivorous and enjoyed hunting wild game. However, even in the earliest days of us becoming We, everyone agreed that all killed animals were to be regarded with the utmost respect. All game needed to be slain with as few blows, arrows, or slashes as possible to minimize the poor creatures' misery. Our hunters would also bless the slain animals' souls as they departed. We saw this as the least We could do.

The soulless ones had a different approach to hunting. This became readily apparent that dusk. They captured a large, gangly creature in a bristled net made of metal. It took two of their biggest men to carry the gentle beast. Maybe it was a type of deer? We weren't sure what kind of animal it was. We had never seen anything like it before, with its impossibly long and slender legs, night-black fur, and pleading round eyes. They then took the petrified creature and dropped it next to a small, loose pile of kindling. Those of us who watched them out of curiosity thought it was a bit strange. They were going to need a lot more kindling if They planned on roasting that whole animal.

One of them, a young woman who saw our puzzled faces, came over to us and whispered, "This is going to be a sacrificed meal. You might want to look away for this next part."

Even those of us who took her advice and looked away could still paint the gruesome scene in our minds. We heard the cracking of bones, popping of joints, and tearing of flesh. We winced at the creature's gurgling screams. We also could not help but listen as the young woman stoically explained what was happening and why:

The sacrifice was necessary to honor new beginnings. A new phase in fellowship. An opportunity for companionship and growth. The men needed to grab and tear off each of the beast's limbs while it was still alive to ensure that the spilled scarlet blood carried life. The limbless creature had to bleed until it choked on its last breath so the men could collect as much of its lifeblood as possible. The blood was collected in wide, smooth black jars to be carried back to the big farm for sacred purposes. By the time the creature was dead, They had gathered enough kindling to start a befitting fire to roast the fresh mound of flesh. Before anyone could eat any of the meat, the creature's inner organs, like the stomach, the brain, and the heart, had to be removed and burned to ashes. Only They could eat this meal according to their holy law. But rest assured, We would have plenty to eat once We reached their big farm. More than plenty to eat.

To be clear, We were not primarily disturbed by the gore of their sacrifice. True, the slaughtering method seemed a bit harsh. But who were We to judge what was sacred to them? We didn't need to understand it to respect their desire to sustain this practice. Perhaps it was central to their faith and culture. No, it was not the gore that disturbed us, though those of us who watched could not sleep for nights afterward. It was the look We saw in their eyes. Their irises were silver bullets, murderous as They ripped the creature apart. Their twisted expressions did not match the reverence of a holy act. That raised our suspicions but not for long. Even after We had finished eating, our thoughts were drowned out by our stomachs' moans.

ROSE

In the same way Adelaide was gifted in connecting with animals, Rose had the golden touch of nurturing plants. She loved the way plants reached for the sun's warmth and light while still deepening their roots in the rich earth. Rose knew that plants, and all living things, had souls and dreams. She was the first one to notice the delicate willow tree by the river with its gentle, guiding presence. And even now, if Rose were here to see how the grass is being forced to swallow the blood from our feet, she would have watered it with her tears. Even the plants share in our suffering.

* * *

In the time before the Great Famine, perhaps surprisingly, Rose lived in a nature-suppressed city, where plants that survived often did so against all odds. While she admired their tenacity, she also yearned to take care of them.

"When I was a little girl," she once explained to us, her gaze of recollection as golden as the rest of her, "I used to dream of having a garden of my own. I had never seen a garden before in person but the idea of a place where plants could grow freely flourished in my imagination. There was no space for a proper garden because scarcity conducted the rhythms of the city. So, instead, I'd try to water all the grass, saplings, and flowers I could find. I wanted them to know I saw them, respected them, and wished them well."

We are fairly certain Rose was one of the first among us. Nobody can remember how or when she became part of us. As far as We know, she was the gentle ambassador that welcomed many of us into this family. It may have even been her idea to create our own language to foster inclusivity. Resisting her characteristic boldness and kindness was impossible. Though she was young, not much older than Adelaide, she had the wisdom of an elder. She never made any direct claims to authority but We revered her as a leader, cherishing her words.

"We all ought to be more like plants," she used to tell us as We rested our feet from the day's journey through the wilderness. "They may not be able to run like We can, but their motion has a balance ours lacks. They long for heights and depths. They stretch both upward and downward, breathing into their own assured sense of place. They know how to grow, to thrive. I pray for the day that will be true for us."

We would be remiss not to mention Rose's captivating beauty. She was angelic but her sunbaked skin, onyx-black hair, and golden eyes were bewitching. Rose considered her appearance a blessing and a curse. When she lived in the city, she often felt the weight of unwanted gazes linger on the small of her back. She had early memories of greedy glances tracing her physique. This was why she loved everyone but only trusted a few chosen people in her life. She loved and trusted all of us but that still did not keep her from tying a leather case holding a dagger around her waist, hidden beneath her clothes. While We were in the wilderness, Rose would often find new ways to sharpen and polish her cherished weapon. She wouldn't let anyone else touch it, which was fine with us. After all, she was the only one among us who knew how to care for and wield it properly.

* * *

As We walked into one of their dining rooms for the first time, ten of their broad-shouldered men stood behind some of the chairs, intently examining our bodies as We filed through the entrance. Other than their quick-scanning eyes, their faces were stiff and lifeless. Their suppressive dullness sharply contrasted the lustrous golden brown of the most beautiful table any of us had ever seen. We knew the table was made of wood but it shone in an almost crystalline way. As We peered closer, We could see that it was covered in intricately carved images of curling, holy flames. Absorbed in admiration, We were hesitant as We sat down around the dining table. We felt We were in the presence of something sacred.

Our awestruck wonder didn't last long. Suddenly, their broad-shouldered men whipped out the ropes They had been holding behind their backs. They made quick work of tying our legs to the chairs, tightly wrapping the ropes around and around, gnawing for blood. Strangely, We were completely rigid as They bound us, too startled to scream. Too desperate for food to make a fuss. Their men slipped out of the dining room once their deed was done.

As soon as the rope tiers left, Rose's hands itched for her dagger. The ropes chafed and burned even then, and Rose wanted to cut them off of us. Something held her back. Perhaps her curiosity. Perhaps her natural inclination to welcome people. Perhaps her fear of jeopardizing our chances of being fed in the future. Nevertheless, while the rest of us were stunned silent by the absurd situation and eagerly waited for our food, Rose was the first to speak to the young woman at the table with us. None of us noticed when she had arrived, as if she had materialized from dense air. She looked like one of their daughters with the same odd skin that glistened in a more-than-human way. And for some reason, she was tied to her chair just like us. After a couple tense, still moments, a few of us recognized her as the girl who had explained the ritual sacrifice.

Rose gently looked into her eyes and smiled. The young woman hesitantly smiled back.

"Hello," Rose began in Common Tongue, her voice warm and inviting. "My name is Rose and this is my family. What's your name?"

"My name is Tabitha," the stranger replied, just above a whisper.

"It's nice to meet you, Tabitha."

"It's nice to meet you, too, Rose. Your family also seems nice."

After a pregnant pause where everyone subtly squirmed under the sting of the ropes, struggling to maintain composure, Tabitha spoke again, this time with more confidence. "Do the ropes around your legs hurt too?"

"Yes. They are rather uncomfortable."

"My parents tell me they are supposed to burn a little," Tabitha explained. "They say the ropes represent all of us being 'tightly bound together by the dream of progress and shared tables.' Progress and sharing require sacrifice, which is what the physical discomfort represents."

"Oh, I see. I am grateful They have welcomed us to their table."

We all stopped shifting, realizing We had no way to be more physically comfortable in the present circumstances. We exchanged pained but hopeful glances. All of this was highly absurd. But at least We would be fed soon.

Tabitha could see the startled looks on our faces. "Don't worry," she said reassuringly. "The food here is wonderful. Everything is so delicious, and your stomachs will be so full and satisfied that you'll forget the ropes are even there. That's what my parents say anyway."

"Well," replied Rose cheerily with a taut smile, "I'm looking forward to all of us sharing this meal together."

She was, in fact, looking forward to it. We all were. But since We knew food was coming, our skin-like desperation began to wear away, allowing a chilled suspicion to seep into us.

"I hope you all are really ready to eat," Tabitha warned. "My parents and their friends will not let us leave until every single morsel of the food is gone."

For our hunger-wounded stomachs, the wait for the food felt like an eternity. But when a few more of their young daughters brought out the platters, the sight of the grandiose feast salved famine-inflicted wounds. We marveled at the unknown delicacies. Adelaide relished in the thick, spiced wild-berry compote, eating it by the spoonful. By her own convictions, Adelaide did not consume any of the meat, which of course came in multiple varieties: Roasted duck, baked chicken, braised beef, and boiled oxtail to name a few. Rose was partial to the decadent, soft bread laced with honey and the voluptuous, leafy salads. Samson, who was truly a lion of a man, followed his more carnivorous inclinations, having at least two portions of each meat type offered. But at Rose's request, Samson also ate a couple servings of some sort of steamed root vegetable. Zenith and Jordan were sure to consume every kind of seafood from the mysterious fried tentacles to the warm, briny fish head stews. Tabitha tentatively took a small bit of everything. Not a single morsel was spared, our hunger finally vanquished. After returning to inspect our cleared plates, the rope tiers freed our tense, bruised legs.

Later that evening, after We ate more than what We ever thought our stomachs could handle, They brought us to our new living quarters. Four identical wooden cabins stood about a fifty-deep-breaths run behind the big house. They divided us into four fairly even groups and ordered us to enter our respective cabins. Each one was filled with three long rows of straw mattresses covered in burlap, which were sure to be more comfortable than dew-moistened ground.

Once We thought They were out of earshot, We all sat on the ground in front of the first cabin to discuss the bizarre circumstances of the day. We spoke in our language, of course. We decided then that We would fall into the rhythm of speaking Common Tongue around the They and our language among ourselves.

Adelaide asked Rose, "What did you think of our first dinner here?"

Rose sighed. "It was . . . unsettling. I really wanted to cut off those ropes with my dagger. It took a lot of restraint to keep myself from writhing in discomfort. I don't trust this place quite yet. I think I like Tabitha though."

"Maybe We'll get to be like plants here." Hope turned Adelaide's eyes a brilliant emerald green. "Maybe this is the place where We'll dream and grow and thrive like you always say."

"Maybe it is." Rose nodded skeptically. "Maybe it is."

* * *

Rose was all too familiar with the weight of the male gaze. In fact, Rose was well aware that the only reason They assigned her to work in the kitchen instead of the field was so the men among them could commit adultery with their eyes. But even during our time wandering the wilderness, Rose would feel a new, quiet warmth wash over her every once and a while. She knew that warmth came from the gentle and longing eyes of an admirer. But Rose was afraid of meeting the gaze of her beholder. She feared her direct acknowledgment would frighten his love away, defiling the sacredness of its secrecy. We all knew who her admirer was long before she did but We promised one another not to tell her directly. True love is something realized between two halves of a shared whole, a bond that is strengthened by the surrounding community, not determined by it.

"I think maybe you should try to look at him," Adelaide advised after hearing Rose's concerns.

"I think so, too," Zenith chimed in, always excited by the potential for blossoming romance. "Once you discover who it is, you'll see, in his eyes, how much he loves."

So, one day not too long before the soulless ones deceived us, Rose felt the warm gaze again and dared to look into the eyes of its source. Her secret hopes were realized in that moment. It was Samson, with his deep bronze skin, thick trunk-like muscles, and glorious coal-black dreadlocks that were akin to a mane. His eyes were a soft gold, his gaze unwaveringly firm and gentle. And Rose and Samson finally discovered what the rest of us already knew. They were destined for each other.

After We were brought to the big farm, They assigned Samson to work in a blacksmith stable not too far away from the big house. Many evenings, after Rose finished her kitchen duties, she snuck away from the big house to come and help Samson with his work. Sometimes, Rose and Samson would craft unexpected trinkets out of scrap metal, making sure nothing went to waste.

Before long, Samson asked Rose to marry him. She had never wanted anything as much as she wanted to be Samson's wife. But on the day They permitted Rose and Samson to jump over a slim, ashy-silver broom, Rose noticed that Samson's suddenly bald head shone like copper in the noonday sun, his magnificent locks gone. We could see the concern in her eyes but she never asked Samson about his locks' disappearance. She thought that maybe shaving one's head for marriage was a custom from his homeland, honoring his past as he leaned into his future with her. But she did not want to risk being wrong about that. Besides, the warm embers of Samson's eyes still glowed in a familiar, loving way, so his new baldness did not make a difference to her. He was still her Samson.

* * *

We admired Rose and Samson's love. Once they were married, Rose did not have to worry about sneaking away to the blacksmith's stable to be with Samson. She could just leave the big house once she was done with her duties for the day. Both Rose and Samson eagerly looked forward to welcoming a child into the world, but after months of trying, it became clear Rose was barren. They, the ones that might still live on the big farm, were disappointed in this reality. Though We had yet to realize this, the main reason why They agreed to Samson and Rose's marriage to begin with was for the production of viable offspring. We doubt They are even capable of appreciating pure human love. Being anything other than exploitative goes against their nature.

"What is a young woman without a functioning womb?" They'd sinisterly remark. "A waste of resources and femininity."

Yet, one day, after Adelaide had passed away and Rose's barrenness had settled into common knowledge, Rose felt the pain of a lustful male gaze on the small of her back while working in the kitchen of the seemingly empty, big house. She told us something about this man's glance felt more violent, sharper. She turned around and looked directly into the man's preying reptilian eyes. He was one of them, with the same more than human glow in his skin, but it was covered with a thin layer of grime.

"And you know what I said to that evil man?" Rose's voice hardened as she recounted the story. She had already made sure Samson was not in the room. "I told him, 'I am sure you think you are entitled to my body and there will not be any evidence or consequences for you since I cannot have children. But I can assure you, if you ever dare to even look at me that way again'—and this is when I took my dagger out of its case—'you will not be able to have children either.'"

Though We always knew Rose to be fearless in everything except for romance, We also understood that this particular boldness was fueled by the gnawing grief over Adelaide's absence. Rose knew Adelaide had died because she so desperately wanted April to live but Rose also knew Adelaide's death could have been prevented. If the soulless ones had cared about Adelaide, had seen her as a human being, she still could have been alive. We knew They had their cure-all medicines but Adelaide was just a defective resource to them. We all were just resources to them, and Rose realized this long before the rest of us did. And We knew in our hearts there would be consequences for Rose's brave defiance.

***

We all remember the night Rose was poisoned. We were all eating at the table, with our legs tied to the chairs as usual, when Tabitha suddenly brought a sweet-smelling, airy-looking pastry out from the kitchen and put it in front of Rose. Tabitha stood next to Rose's chair. It was strange having to look up to see her face.

"It's called a cream puff," Tabitha explained in response to our puzzled faces. "My parents said it's for your birthday, Rose."

We should have wanted to ask many questions then: How did They know it was Rose's birthday? None of us know when our birthdays are, so why was that day of all days Rose's birthday? In hindsight, it was all suspicious, but instead of rightfully interrogating the situation with exchanged glances, We all stared at the luxurious cream puff with our mouths agape.

Rose was naturally hesitant. "I am not sure I want to eat something so beautiful."

Samson lovingly placed his hand on her shoulder. "I think you should eat it. A beautiful dessert for a beautiful woman."

"Do you want some?" Rose gestured with her knife that she'd cut the cream puff in half to share.

Tabitha interjected. "Actually, my parents said They only want you to eat it. It's their gift to you."

"But Samson and I are one," Rose protested. "That's what we believe marriage is about."

"It's okay, Rose," Samson consoled. "It is probably for the best that I don't eat more dessert anyway."

When Rose looked into Samson's eyes, something in her heart stilled, her nerves dissipating. Truthfully, she wanted to eat the whole cream puff but she never enjoyed thinking of her own desires. Samson often had to remind Rose to put herself first, insisting it would not make her any less loving or beautiful or selfless.

Rose ate every sweet and lethal bite.

Rose must have fallen asleep for the last time with a smile. Her body was cold and rigid in the morning. Even in death she was beautiful, her skin still golden, her inner radiance eternal. It took everything within us to hold back mourning wails as They stiffly carried her body away, as if it were merely a sack of coal. In the same way We had longed to have a funeral for Adelaide, We wished We could have at least buried Rose in the richest soils on the big farm. She belonged anywhere there would be new growth. But They showed no sympathy or emotion as They ordered us to our daily duties.

When Samson realized Rose was gone, he lost his sense of self.

W E

We still do not know how We should feel about their visitors. As We think of them now, our guts stir with a gurgling mixture of disgust and pity. On one hand, the visitors were just as bad as They were. If anything, the visitors were worse, suggesting new forms of cruelty as if they were bread recipes. On the other hand, it soon became clear to us that the visitors longed for approval from the They. How sad. Perhaps the visitors were so eager to degrade us to create a façade of strength that They would value. The visitors wanted to be deemed worthy of partnering with the They for the same twisted mission. Little do any of them know how blind they were and perhaps still are.

We remember the first time their visitors came. We had arrived at the big farm not too long before. Adelaide was still alive and We were just starting to fall into our new rhythm: wake up at the sun's first pink ray, walk to the big house to eat small bowls of nuts and dried fruits for breakfast as They watched us, work until dusk, have our legs tied to the chairs as We ate an elaborate dinner, be released to our cabins where We would whisper about our strange day, clean and dress our rope burns, and sleep on coarse straw mattresses. But the day their visitors came called for a different routine.

First, They woke us up before dawn with a blast from a growling horn. Startled, We were corralled outside our cabins and steered to the river. Standing as far away from the bank as possible while still staying vigilant, They told us to bathe. We were hesitant as We waded into the murky, cold waters. They had commanded us to go into this river before for a different reason. The currents surged with our fresh memories of panic. While We tried our best to remain calm, They laughed as They tossed brown bars of soap to us.

Maybe this is some sort of game They like?

Each of their guffaws sounded like the screech of a rusting door hinge. Every once in a while, a chuckle would become a violent, wet cough.

Maybe They all have colds? Adelaide knows the recipe for herb tea that can help with that.

It was strange to see them in such good spirits. As They handed out ragged towels, They told us that They had visitors coming.

"Make sure everything, absolutely everything, is clean and organized," They ordered, their voices emotionless. "Let nothing, not a single thing, go to waste."

Their visitors arrived at high noon. We had spent the morning making final preparations: pulling weeds from the fields, scrubbing the wooden floors, and sweeping debris from the long, stone-paved path to the big house's front steps. As soon as They heard the deep thuds of hooves and sharp creaking wheels of their guests' carriages, They had us line up straight along either side of the path and strain our faces with taut smiles. Their visitors took their sweet time getting out of their carriages, making each still second all the more agonizing. Our cheeks were throbbing and We were sweating profusely in the noon heat. But as They had demanded, We looked like perfectly happy, healthy, and hearty workers. And to some extent, that's what We were at the time, grinning in our naivety.

As the visitors finally strolled toward us, We had to swallow gasps of amazement. The visitors looked just like the They. The same long strides. The same steel-bullet eyes. The same stone-like faces. The only discernible difference was that their metallic skin was a shiny, deep gray while the They had skin the color of polished gold. Perhaps the visitors were distant relatives? A few of the guests' stronger-looking men carried large forest-green chests that were presumably filled with gifts. They refused to make eye contact with any of us but We could feel their gazes trace our bodies. Relief washed over us when one of the They finally opened the door to welcome the visitors into the big house.

"Welcome to our home, dear brothers," the They man bellowed. "May Fullness burn within you all, guiding you all in light, warmth, and growth."

The visitors gently bowed their heads as they received the blessing. "May it also burn within you."

We thought They were going to make us tend to their guests. But oddly, after They welcomed the visitors into the big house shortly after noon, the rest of our daily routine remained untouched. We were sent back to work in our respective stations and called as usual to be tied to our chairs for dinner. Those of us who worked in the kitchen, like Rose and Zenith, noticed the visitors and the They spent most of the day somewhere in the impenetrable heart of the big house. Rose and Zenith weren't able to tell where They all had gone but they heard metallic laughter echoing through wooden walls.

We all assumed the visitors were going to stay longer but they only stayed at the big farm for one night. The soulless ones woke us up before dawn with the growling horn again so We could see the visitors off. Thank God They did not make us bathe in the frigid river again. The guests were all set to leave by the time half of the red sun peered over the horizon. Some of the visitors' men carried many of the smooth black jars We had seen the They fill with blood in the wilderness.

One of the They, a particularly sharp-eyed man, stepped toward a jar carrier and asked, "May we trust you with the power of this lifeblood?"

The jar carrier slightly bowed his head in reverence. "You may, just as we trust you with the power of the elixirs."

As the visitors loaded their carriages, We noticed when that same jar carrier keenly measured Rose and Samson's proportions with his stare. He turned to the They man, inquiring, "How much would you be willing to trade for a male and a female of your fleshed ones?"

Then, with surprising vitriol, the They man spat, "We will not trade them for anything. They are our fleshed ones. They are part of our household. You must find your own elsewhere."

At first, the visitor seemed hurt by the sudden aggression, a pained grimace flashing across his face. But his expression quickly settled into something highly unnerving—a smirk.

"Very well," he replied somewhat coyly. "We shall go on our way then. May Fullness burn within you all, guiding you all in light, warmth, and growth."

The They man returned the blessing with cold formality. "May it also burn within you."

SAMSON

Maybe stopping wasn't the wisest idea. Since We are not running at the moment, our relaxing muscles are beginning to feel the unkind cold of the night air. When We run, the memories in our bones, as hallowed as they are, still feel as light as the rest of our bodies. But as We settle here, albeit briefly, without the consistent drawing motion toward what We might call freedom, the memories settle with us, heavy as they stir around in our bones' marrow. The pain that comes with this is different from that of our strained, sore muscles; gashed, bleeding feet; or throbbing, mosquito-bitten skin. This pain is adjacent to hunger's pain, an acute awareness of absence's presence.

We are struggling to build a fire on the moist ground. The last time We were all here together, before the deception, Samson was our master of the flame. He could make a spark leap out from between any two stones when he struck them together. As if fire were in his veins. As if smoldering embers were in his eyes. And remembering Samson's warm and life-giving gaze, which was extinguished after Rose's death, our own eyes fill with tears as if stung by smoke.

No, stopping was the wisest idea. We cannot afford to shy away from this grief. We know this. Samson did not shy away from it as he mourned Rose. He tenderly embraced it, almost as if it were Rose herself. Almost. And watching that man of fire and metal let his tears water the earth, a mourning melody ebbing from his lips, was something of tragic beauty. Of a heart prostrated to love and the weight of memory. He is our inspiration now. We need to grant ourselves this moment to feel, to keel over in our shared agony. To cry. To wail. Even if only for a moment. If We deny that the memories and their pain are in us as We move, the pervasive ache will ravage our minds and muscles, paralyzing us forever.

Fine. Let the wind castigate us for stopping. Let it try to pierce between joint and marrow and strip the memories right out of us. The wind will not succeed. It may carry our bodies as We run but that is all We will allow. Our memories will stay rooted in us. We will fight for that. Without this chosen moment of stillness amid motion, of feeling the memories' weight, We would never be able to move as ourselves again. We would forget how to be human. We would turn into the They.

* * *

Not too long after We met Adelaide in the forest, We saw Samson's warm gaze for the first time. We were traveling through the desert by night since the day's heat was often merciless. That night had no moon. The thin clouds had dissipated. The stars were dim and distant. Thankfully, the sky was already beginning to whisper the promise of a new day, its deep blue-black filling with homely shades of red, orange, and gold.

The sun had yet to rise, though, and it was still dark enough for us to see what looked like a small fire in the distance. We walked toward it, following Rose's lead. She often took the risk of assuming that those We encountered would be friends and not foes. As We approached the fire, We could see the figure of an impossibly large man kneeling close to the flames.

Goodness. If he is this large during this time of scarcity, imagine how big he must be when he is properly fed.

Some of us wondered if this man was proof that giants roamed the earth.

He must have seen us coming but he also appeared to be in some sort of trance, studying the dancing flames. Rose, fearless as ever, stepped closer and closer until she was only a breath away from the fire, directly across from the man. When Rose's face was completely illuminated by the fire, the man flickered out of his daze, and the embers of his huge eyes smoldered. Perhaps it was because of his broad shoulders. Perhaps it was because of his long, coal-black dreadlocks. Perhaps it was because of his gentle smile or the sudden heat of the sun stretching from the horizon behind him. But something We had never seen before happened.

Rose blushed.

"Hi," Rose said in Common Tongue, her tone cool. "My name is Rose, and this is my family. What is your name, sir?"

"Sir? You flatter me with formality, miss." The man chuckled softly, his voice a robust baritone. "Please, just call me Samson."

"Well, sir, I mean, Samson, do you by chance know where We might be able to rest? We are new to this part of the desert. You must know how deadly the heat becomes, and it has been harder on some of us than others. We really need to find shade for the day."

"Say no more," Samson stood up swiftly, revealing that Rose, who We had considered tall, only came up to the base of his chest. A giant roaming the earth indeed. "There is a fading yet viable oasis not too far from here. I can take you all there. Just follow me. We need to be quick though. There isn't much time before the morning sun fully rises." Still stunned by Samson's presence, We all followed him, struggling to keep up with his long strides.

"Will We be able to find food at this oasis?" Rose piped in after a lull of spellbound silence.

Samson nodded thoughtfully. "There isn't much, but there should be enough for us all to subsist. Some leafy trees. Some succulents to suck or chew on for water. Some locusts during the day and some crickets at night. Maybe all of us will be fortunate in finding a few fruits. While you all rest, I'll catch locusts and roast them over a fire."

"Are you sure you want to build a fire during the day? The sun already feels like it'll be particularly unforgiving."

"I appreciate your concern, Rose, but I'll be fine. Trust me. I deal with fire at all times of the day. The heat doesn't bother me much anyway."

* * *

Samson naturally became one of us. He had no need for an invitation, subtle or otherwise. He was drawn in by his God-given love of helping people and by Rose's liquid gold beauty. He fell into our circadian rhythms, his body tiring when We grew weary. But many days or nights, depending on which landscape We traveled and what times We all rested, he fought against his flesh to stay awake to tend to the fire.

Like Adelaide and Jordan, Samson did not like to talk much about his past. He only ever told all of us a couple of things. Perhaps he shared more with Rose. First, Samson explained how he was separated from his family of origin by a wild sandstorm, one of the Great Famine's earliest birth pains. Second, Samson proudly remembered his father as the family's ultimate master of the flame. Samson wanted to be our master of the flame to honor his father's legacy.

He wouldn't say anything else when We tried to ask more questions. We eventually knew to leave it well enough alone.

Every once in a while, Jordan would keep Samson company as he watched the flames. Samson and Jordan's relational dynamic was similar to the one between Rose and Adelaide. We were all family to one another but they treated each other like close siblings. One night, We overheard one of Samson and Jordan's brotherly conversations.

"You know, Samson," Jordan said with a teasing raised eyebrow, "You sure do look at the fire intently. Almost as intently as you look at Rose."

Samson pushed Jordan's shoulder in jest but Jordan still winced a little bit. Samson forgot how strong he was sometimes. Samson chuckled softly. "Well, Jordan, you're not wrong. I often pray that maybe, just maybe, Rose and I would have sparks someday. You know, like the ones between you and Zenith."

"Oh, come on. It's not like that between me and Zenith. We go way back, though, like to the times before the famine."

"Okay. You might want to tell that to your face whenever you look at her."

Jordan rolled his eyes. "You're just trying to change the subject. Do you think you'll ever just tell Rose how you feel?"

"I don't know. Maybe. I have thought about saying something to her. But even when I've garnered up the courage to do it, I can't. Even just looking at her, it's like trying to describe the sun at dawn. Words don't suffice, you know?"

"Actually, I don't know. I've never felt that way about anyone, but maybe the words will come to you. Or maybe you'll be lucky and something beyond words will draw you two together." Jordan seemed startled by his own insight but then a familiar smirk crept across his face. "I just hope whatever it is happens soon, because that sappy look on your face is making me cringe."

Samson pushed Jordan's shoulder and Jordan winced again. They both laughed and watched the flames until sleep finally overtook them.

* * *

After We were brought to their big house, They took a liking to Samson right away. And We don't blame them for this. They must have thought Samson was a perfect work specimen. A stud. Because of his strength and his natural gift with fire, They strategically sent him to work as a blacksmith. Unsurprisingly, Samson fell in love with blacksmithing.

"There's something so beautiful about it," he'd explain to us while dressing yet another burn wound. "There's nothing like seeing new things, useful things, emerge from heat and sweat and metal and flame and strength and mind, you know?"

And he wasn't wrong. It *was* beautiful, and he became addicted to perfecting the craft. He was also addicted to inviting Rose into the blacksmith's stable. She'd sneak away from the big house to come and help him. By the time the soulless ones had deceived us, plenty of sparks had lit between Samson and Rose. Their shared time in the blacksmith stable further kindled their affection until it burned surely and steadily. We cannot emphasize enough how beautiful it was to see the two of them together, their love shining like something divine.

* * *

As We stayed on their big farm and had a steady intake of their elaborate cuisine, We all became physically stronger. We could no longer see our sharp ribs protruding from our translucent skin. But Samson seemed to almost double in size, his chest bulging and bronze muscles rippling. Now that he was well-fed, Samson was stronger than three of their oxen. To be clear, he was more than brute strength. He had the stature of Goliath but the heart of David. Needless to say, Samson was not one to be underestimated.

One day, while Samson was walking from the blacksmith stable, he overheard the grumbling of four young men of the They. They were dragging a heavy black chest toward the big house. Samson could decipher something about trading copies with their visitors for other goods from the Embers but that didn't seem to be anything important. Samson's attention was piqued when the young men slandered us.

One of them boasted that "the fleshed ones weren't even worthy of touching this chest." Another concurred and asserted that We were "mostly useless, except for doing mindless tasks." The third one said We were "just skin and bones moving." The fourth nodded and shared that he still "wouldn't mind letting his hands caress the curves of the fleshed women. Especially that one called Rose."

Samson found himself briskly walking over to them and stopping a breath away. He tilted his head down to look each of the four young men in their steel-bullet eyes. Then, without a word, Samson picked up the chest as if it were as light as morning air and placed it right outside the big house's front door.

"They were young men. Really young," Samson recalled as he told us the story that evening. "Perhaps that's why They were so arrogant. I hope I was able to give those four a subtle lesson in humility."

* * *

The rest of the They were pleased overall with Samson and his work. We're sure that he proved to be more valuable of an asset than They had initially anticipated. But They still had one thorn-like point of contention—Samson's dreadlocks.

"They say that my hair might catch fire while I'm in the blacksmith stable," Samson would complain, "but They don't understand the fire like Rose and I do. If you are careful and nimble, you don't have to be scared of the flames. You just have to respect the fire like any other breathing thing. Besides, I'm a grown man. I can handle myself."

And as a grown man, Samson soon developed a burning desire to handle more than just himself. We all knew he wanted to marry Rose. So, when he garnered up the courage to ask them permission to do it, none of us were shocked. However, everything still had to be done according to their rules,.

"We will oblige your request under one condition, Samson," They said in a droning hum. "We must shave off your dreadlocks."

The choice was easy for Samson.

He followed them into a room at the seemingly impenetrable heart of the big house. It contained the largest furnace Samson had ever seen, the flames greedily licking at its sides. But that wasn't even the most unsettling part: The fire was *violet*. A deep and painfully violent blaze of violet.

What type of fire was this? Maybe it turned this color from a sacred kind of fuel?

It took everything in Samson's power to maintain his composure as They pressed their razor blade to his head. He later confessed he might have shed a single tear. Who could blame him? Samson was losing a part of himself.

"I sure am going to miss my dreadlocks in the winter," he tried to joke as he gestured toward his copper-smooth bald head. We could still see a hue of blue sadness in his eyes. He had made sure that Rose wasn't in the room. "But hair grows back. There's only one Rose."

After They had finished shaving off his locks, They threw the long oil-slicked ropes of hair into the ravenous furnace fire. "We are just making sure nothing goes to waste," They said.

Samson never told Rose how or why his locks disappeared. Rose had already begun to question their surroundings. Knowing the soulless ones had burned Samson's dreadlocks would only heighten her suspicions. Worry was not going to cast its shadow on Samson and Rose's new married life. Samson would work to guarantee that by any means necessary, even if it took secrets. Little did Samson know that not too much later, Rose would keep secrets to protect Samson, too. If Samson found out about her threatening encounter with one of the They, if he heard her describe the grimy man's greedy gaze, Samson's anger would have violently flared up. The desire to avenge Rose would have blinded him and, perhaps, made him do something reckless. Samson often forgot how strong he was. So, there were secrets between them. Secrets that burdened Samson's and Rose's respective consciences. Secrets they both kept for the sake of the other. Secrets We honored and maintained as their family. Whatever it took to protect Samson, Rose, and their relationship.

Despite Rose's barrenness, They still wanted to take full advantage of Samson, their prized stud. So, They presented him with two options. Samson could annul the marriage to freely sleep with fertile young women. Or he could stay married to Rose while still freely sleeping with fertile young women. Either way, his seed was going to produce offspring. Simple. Samson refused both options.

"I'm a married man," he protested. "Before jumping over the broom, I vowed not to part with Rose until death. If Rose can't have a child, I won't have one either."

Oh, you poor boy. You poor, pure-hearted, love-blind boy. How could you have been so naive?

* * *

After Rose was poisoned, Samson hardened like quenched metal. As They carried her body away, Samson was motionless, his eyes tracing the space where Rose used to sleep next to him. We tried to console him, stifling expressions of grief for his sake. Jordan sat next to Samson and kept him company like he did when We were still wandering. We all stayed with Samson until They came and dragged us to our respective workstations. Yet, as he lumbered toward the blacksmith stable, We saw something dangerous in Samson's usually warm gaze. It had become scorching hot with anger.

Later that day, under the cloak of nightfall, Samson snuck out of the cabin. A few of us, including Jordan, heard Samson moving around and trailed close behind him through the biting, cold air. We weren't good at being discreet, so Samson turned around, his stare crazed, and he said with an unfamiliar blazing edge, "Fine. You all can follow me, but only if you're ready for rebellion." Filled with raw rage ourselves, We continued to follow him, still struggling to keep up with his long yet stealthy strides. He brought us to the arsenal, and with one powerful push, Samson broke the door open. Startled and spellbound, We watched as Samson picked up the same gun They had used to kill Adelaide's beloved April, stepped outside, and pointed the gun straight toward the misery-black sky.

"Rose was right all along," Samson's growling whisper bellowed into the still night. He might as well have been yelling. "They lied to us. They're using us. They've destroyed their sense of humanity. And because We are so desperate for food in these times, We are letting them destroy ours, too." His arm trembled as his finger found the trigger. "This gunshot will be a declaration of our freedom, of our chance to reclaim some of what has been taken from us. This is for Adelaide. This is for Rose." His face shone with a threatening intensity as ferocious tears blurred his vision. And We were caught up in the swell of it all.

But Samson could not bring himself to fire the weapon. The smoldering embers in his eyes were suddenly extinguished. We watched, as if in slow motion, as Samson dropped the gun, crumbling as he followed it to the ground. He buried his face into the dirt and wept. Unabashedly. Everything else he had said and done that night has been under the hushed veil of secrecy. But seeing him wail then, shaking violently as he sobbed, was like watching the earth swallow a mountain. Samson's rage had become sorrow and shame. Sorrow for all he had lost. Shame for his capacity for destruction. Nothing was intelligible then, everyone reduced to groanings too deep for words. Or at least for words alone.

For when Samson finally lifted his head from the dirt, a mourning melody ebbed from his lips:

How will the dawn come
now that you're gone?
How will the earth drink the morning dew?
How will my fire burn on
now that I don't have you?
You were the light I saw by.
You painted days golden hues.
And no matter where I was planted,
you were the reason why I grew.

Though I may never be my full self again,
at least not the "me" you helped me become,
show me how to honor your memory
each time I rise before the sun.

Samson's soul soon followed Rose to heaven. He dragged his body across the fields to the blacksmith's stable. Samson only ate a fourth of what he used to. He reluctantly chewed on the root vegetables Rose had encouraged him to eat. Grief carved away his flesh startlingly quickly. He was still muscular but We could trace his bones through his dulling skin. His gaze became dark and vacant, only brightening ever so slightly when he heard Rose's name.

After a few days, Samson would hide during meals so he wouldn't have to continue to face the last place he and Rose ate together. At first, They would hunt him down and tie his legs extra tight. They couldn't afford to lose such a valuable asset and They realized how rapidly Samson was deteriorating. They didn't understand that Samson was already gone. Desperate to see Samson's brute strength restored, They bound his hands at the dining table and had one of their young women feed Samson the meat he once enjoyed. He regained some physical strength but it would all be for nothing. Samson soon outwitted the They, lying down in the woods at dinner time, camouflaging himself with mud so They couldn't find him. That was his final method of rebellion.

When They told us They found his body in the black-smith's stable, saying that he died from smoke inhalation a couple weeks after Rose passed, none of us were surprised. Samson had swallowed too much smoke. If anything, We were amazed that his body carried on for as long as it did. Perhaps humming the mourning song to himself helped salve his wounded heart for a short time, but without Rose, nothing would ever be enough.

When We first learned of Samson's death, just like with Adelaide and Rose, We longed to properly bury him, to have the time to mourn losing him with his gentleness and strength. Then, We realized that Samson would not have wanted to be buried on their big farm. Especially in his final days, he didn't want anything to do with them or what They offered us. He knew We didn't belong there. But even after he was gone, We still weren't willing to admit that to ourselves. If We didn't belong on the big farm, where did We belong? Surely it wasn't out in the Great Famine–stricken wilderness. We didn't have Samson's resolve. We still couldn't see beyond our full dinner plates. We couldn't see beyond our fear.

* * *

We weren't able to start a fire tonight. Even as We moved away from the riverbed, the ground was still too damp. None of us have Samson's gift. We've decided to run again, knowing the movement would warm us, racing toward the light and heat of sunrise. As the wind carries us and We acknowledge and cling to the memories in our bones, We sing the final lines of Samson's song:

> Though We may never be our full selves again,
> at least not the "We" you each helped us become,
> show us how to honor your memory
> each time We rise before the sun.

Their guests came again. So much had changed for us since their first visit. We had lost Adelaide, Rose, and Samson by then. Our hands were calloused from work and our hearts were hardened by grief. Dawns were no longer lush with warm shades of pink and gold. Or maybe they were. But for us, the world's beauty was obscured by a dense, muted blue fog. We went through the motions of our mechanized routine, obeying almost everything, questioning almost nothing. Some of us could still taste rebellion on the tips of our tongues but We only dared to say anything in hushed tones in our cabins at night. Even then, We uttered empty words. Words as empty as We were.

So, when They woke us with the growling horn yet again, We thoughtlessly followed them to the river, bathed as They kept vigil from afar, cleaned most of the big house, cleared the path, and lined up to greet the visitors at high noon. Just like before. But We could tell something was different. For one, the They were not in good spirits this time around. We wondered if They were still angered by what had happened before—when the visitors wanted to purchase what They considered theirs. Once the visitors left their carriages and stood on the big house's front steps, a few of the They came to the door and opened it. They did not welcome the guests inside.

The gruff They man who had rejected the trade of the "fleshed ones" moved forward and curtly said, "May the Fullness burn within you all."

The visitors' leader, the vocal jar carrier from before, retorted, "Brother, are we not worthy of a full blessing?"

"Do not call me 'brother,'" the They man replied, his voice sharpening. "You are not worthy. You blasphemed Fullness with your sacrilegious request. But no matter. We must handle business."

The visitors looked at us warily and asked if they could go inside to discuss logistics in private. The They flatly refused. Everything that had to happen should be done out in the open, They reasoned. They did not want to stay in the company of blasphemers longer than necessary. Any façade of cordiality disintegrated.

"Very well," the guests' leader conceded. "We will keep this brief. Your violet fire has begun to feast on your common sense."

"You speak as if your *green* fire hasn't burned your minds to ashes," the They man spat. "Someone hurry and bring the chest so we can rid ourselves of these imbeciles."

We watched as four young men of the They dutifully dragged the same black chest Samson had carried with such ease. The visitors also brought a similar chest forward but theirs was a deep blood red.

"This new elixir better multiply our fleshed ones as promised," the They man warned, "or this will mark the end of our agreement."

"It will," the guests' leader insisted. "Its power is worthy of being exchanged for sacred knowledge. Apparently worthier than we are of a full blessing. By the glory of the Embers, it will bring you what you deserve."

The trade was quick. The They placed the red chest in the big house and the visitors hoisted the black chest into their largest carriage. The sun had yet to leave its peak in the sky by the time the transaction was over. Perhaps the brevity was for the best.

Once the guests left, They sent us back to work in our respective stations. Unlike the They, We were glad the visitors had come. Their arrival had broken up our dismal monotony and reminded us of the world beyond the isolated big farm. We then spent the rest of that day marveling at our imagined strangeness of rainbow-colored fires. We remembered the look in Samson's smoldering eyes as he described watching the violet fire swallow his beloved locks. It was a wrestling blend of fear, sadness, and wonder. A multifaceted gaze of awe. We had just assumed that the unique violet hue was from burning some unknown holy fuel. But could that be true for the visitors' green fire too? Did the difference between green and violet really matter? Perhaps the distinction was about more than just fuel. Perhaps it was more about assertions of beauty and power.

ZENITH

We have been running, almost climbing, a steep hill for most of the day. This, of course, is good. Even in the time before the Great Famine, We each knew that it is wiser to seek the higher ground in any and all ways possible. Our legs would heartily disagree. As someone who was no stranger to new heights, Zenith would have been the first to remind us of that old proverb.

We have only stopped for a break once today around noon. It was the shortest one We've had since the genesis of our exodus. We barely allowed ourselves enough time to sigh. Well, perhaps that is a slight exaggeration. We were able to throw something in our mouths, sigh, and then go on our way. This increasing brevity is for the best though. The farther We are from their big farm, the more We can hope that their condemning laziness will thwart their desires or attempts to pursue us. We constantly relay this reasoning to our aching muscles that want to collapse in rebellion. But our minds and souls are fixed on the resolve of freedom, accepting our newfound identities as fugitives. Our bodies obey our ultimate will by God's grace alone.

As We carve ourselves into this scene, We cannot help but think that this moment is a contradiction. It is evening now and the world is hushed by twilight. The wind is probably off meditating somewhere. The air is calm and quiet from the setting sun's lullaby. Yet We continue to run at a desperate, hurtling speed. Surely this makes sense given our circumstances. We do not know where We are beyond what We can see. We are not sure whether They are following us. And admittedly, We are not running *toward* anywhere on this Great Famine–stricken earth. Just *away* from the They. As far away from them as We can get. That much is certain. That, the persistent throb of our beloved lost ones' absence, and not much else. And yet, no one would detect any uncertainty in our strides. It is strange moving through this stillness. But here We are, slicing through the stasis of this moment. Darting forward, one foot in front of the other. We can almost see Zenith running with us, her gait familiar with inclines, and hear her chanting her favorite phrase in her characteristically measured way. One of us begins to say it aloud and soon We all join in:

"Survive to be alive and thrive. Survive to be alive and thrive. Survive to be alive and thrive."

* * *

Survive to be alive and thrive. Zenith whispered this phrase to herself as she rowed toward coastal shores, away from where her home island had once been. She explained this to us soon after We met her on a beach near a broken canoe.

She spoke quietly but firmly, her voice filled with grief and resolve, wavering but never breaking. "My goodness. You all should have seen those waves. They were . . . they were . . . *angry.* Like nothing I'd ever seen before. I was almost paralyzed by their size and ferocity. And if one of God's angels hadn't pushed my shoulder to snap me out of my daze, I-I would have drowned. Simple as that. Simple. I would have drowned. But something happened and I felt myself moving, moving, and moving until I was in a canoe, rowing desperately away from the waves and my home, an island with the highest mountain peak imaginable. I rowed as quickly as

I could, but you know, I couldn't help but look back. I just couldn't. And I saw it. I saw the waves and the ocean floor swallowing up my island, leaving nothing but the top of the mountain peak breaking through the surface. I used to climb that mountain all the time. I was born near the top of that peak, you know. That was the last thing I saw before another angry wave came and capsized my canoe."

Even then, We could tell she was quiet by nature. Something in the tremor of her voice, her cadence, told us that. But long stretches of loneliness can cause someone to be either more guarded or more vulnerable. For Zenith, it was clearly the latter. And our hearts swelled as We heard her recount her journey. Rose and Adelaide were moved to tears. All of us had experienced the loss of our homelands to some degree but few of us could relate to witnessing their complete apocalyptic destruction. Zenith further explained how she miraculously managed to survive, flip over the boat, and row through the ocean, thankfully finding a small island every once in a while, for food and drinkable water.

"This canoe lasted an impossibly long time," she bragged. "I've lost track of how long I've been out on the water, but it just broke on a jagged rock as I rowed to this shore. Nothing short of a miracle."

Rose had tears streaming down her face but she kept her voice calm as she gently placed a hand on each of Zenith's broad shoulders. Rose begged, "Zenith, you must stay with us. And if you don't want to do that, then We will stay with you. Either way, you are part of us now. You've been alone out on that unforgiving water for too long."

Then, Zenith leaned into Rose's chest and softly sobbed. We could see the wearied tension in Zenith's shoulders. It had been too long. Zenith shook as she sobbed harder, Rose firmly holding her up. Far too long.

* * *

Zenith, in her quiet and persistent manner, wove herself into the fabric of our family. As she floated among us, her presence was soothing. Perhaps that was because, despite her extraordinary journey, Zenith carried herself in such an ordinary way. We mean that as lovingly as possible, of course. She wasn't a walking willow like Adelaide. She didn't gleam a sun-kissed gold like Rose. She couldn't summon fire and strength like Samson. But sky and ocean blues pooled in Zenith's eyes. Freckles were dusted across her cheeks. Her loose, curly hair was cropped short to her scalp. A practical style indeed. And although she was young, probably somewhere between Adelaide and Rose's ages, her tan skin was worn by sun, wind, and sea salt, making her look older than her years.

Something about Zenith was still striking but she was the most approachable person of us all. She learned our language with ease but still didn't talk much. However, she often hovered near lively conversations, listening intently. When she did speak, Zenith would give us quick glimpses of the life she'd lived before the Great Famine, before she joined our We. Climbing her island's mountain to its highest peak where she was born. Learning to be the fastest child swimmer to win summer festival races. Gathering fruits from the tallest trees to squeeze out their pucker-sweet juice.

Zenith reminded us to remember. "We aren't who We are without where We've been," she'd say. "Those memories are a matter of survival."

Though Zenith did enjoy Rose and Adelaide's company, she didn't become overly close with anyone for a while. She gave equal attention to each of us. We all felt safe around her. But when We later met Jordan on a beach further along the coast, Zenith was instantly drawn to him. Jordan, being a quick-witted and charismatic person, relished in Zenith's attention. Their connection was clearly mutual. At first, We all assumed that a quiet romance stirred between Zenith and Jordan, something akin to the sparks between Rose and Samson. But it wasn't quite that. At times, We saw Zenith rest her head on Jordan's shoulder, a gesture seemingly reserved for him alone. Other times, We caught Jordan trying to count the shades of blue in Zenith's eyes under his breath. He would usually count up to thirteen or fourteen but everyone knew there were way more than that. Again, this wasn't romance. If We asked either of them about their dynamic, they would both roll their eyes and dismiss us.

Rose and Adelaide especially enjoyed teasing Zenith about Jordan.

"So, Zenith," Rose playfully began as the three of them were slicing up fruit We had picked from the beach. "You know how you were right about me and Samson?"

"You were definitely right," Adelaide chimed in, nodding.

"Well, now it's my turn to be right about you and Jordan," Rose proudly declared.

"Please, not this again." Zenith rolled her eyes. "Trust me. Jordan and I are really just friends."

"Oh, really?" Adelaide quipped. "You might want to tell that to your face whenever you look at him."

"Listen, you two," Zenith said, her tone a bit more serious but still kind, "I know you mean well, but there is nothing like that between me and Jordan. Besides, aren't We all a little bit too busy surviving to be thinking about things like relationships?"

Adelaide gently placed her hand on Zenith's shoulder. "I know you care a lot about surviving, Zenith. We all do. But maybe deepening your relationship with Jordan can lean into being alive and thriving, you know?"

Rose gently placed her hand on Zenith's other shoulder. "I'd listen to Adelaide if I were you. She's wise beyond her years."

Zenith shook her head and laughed. "You two can be so ridiculous sometimes."

But after quite a while of badgering her with questions, Zenith did eventually tell us why she was first drawn to Jordan. He embodied an echo from Zenith's past. Apparently, Jordan grew up on an island not too far away from Zenith. His people and her people would regularly engage in trade. That was of course until the Great Famine started and all ties were severed. Zenith and Jordan might have even crossed paths during their childhoods. Maybe their similar origins forged their unique bond.

* * *

After the deception, which happened a few moons after We met Jordan, the soulless ones had trouble assigning a role to Zenith. This was not because she lacked the skills necessary to do any particular job. Quite the contrary. Zenith was a jack of all trades, so They argued over where she would be the most useful. Since conflict resolution is not their strong suit,

Zenith found herself oscillating between multiple roles in the big house and across the big farm. Sometimes she would slice vegetables or wash dishes with Rose in the kitchen. Other times she would shovel horse dung with Adelaide in the stables. And occasionally, Zenith would sort fish on the river dock, seeing Jordan whenever the boat came in with a fresh catch. That was probably her favorite job. But usually, They sent Zenith up the hill to the vast apple orchards, where she was responsible for tending to and harvesting the fruit in large baskets. She often had to climb the trees to pick the highest apples. She liked the orchards well enough.

"I like the way the orchard air smells," Zenith would say thoughtfully when We asked her about her job there. "It smells like warmth, soft earth and, well, apples. My home island didn't have any apples. Still, I know that Rose would love the orchards much more than I do. I would rather be on the river dock."

Some nights after dinner, despite the raw rope burns on their legs, Zenith and Jordan would stealthily run to the river and slip into its icy cold water. They would swim and swim and swim together, sometimes until dawn, trying to hide the fatigue of their muscles throughout the rest of the day. We pretended not to notice their secret excursions. We also pretended not to see Jordan whenever he used a pen and the scrap paper he took from the big house to write down Zenith's coined phrases. It was his favorite way to tease her. He called the phrases "Zenithisms," which of course only made Zenith roll her eyes and blush. We knew that Zenith and Jordan would deny everything if We tried to ask about anything. So, We kept quiet. Even Adelaide, Rose, and Samson, who fought back every urge to lovingly tease Zenith and Jordan. Some things are better off being known but unsaid.

And yet, it soon became so clear that even the owners of the big farm noticed the connection between Zenith and Jordan. A while after Rose and Samson were married and Rose's barrenness was known, They arranged for Zenith and Jordan to be married. Their announcement of this new ruling was particularly tense. One evening during dinner, when our legs were tied to the chairs, Zenith and Jordan were ordered to sit next to each other by a tall and grave-looking soulless one. Their legs were tied extra tightly, both Zenith and Jordan stifling grimaces. Tabitha wasn't there. Just the grave one of them and the stone-faced rope tiers, their metallic, more-than-human skin gleaming.

The stern giant leaned down until he was a breath away from Zenith's face. "You will marry that boy," he demanded with a sword-sharp snap of his teeth, glaring over at Jordan, "and you will produce viable offspring or else. No more of this barren nonsense." He looked Zenith straight in the eye and growled, "Don't be a waste."

All of this seemingly came out of nowhere to Zenith but something had happened to prompt this. It was one of Jordan's secrets that We kept for him. More secrets for the sake of protecting a relationship. Zenith and Jordan jumped over the slim silver broom the afternoon following that dinner. They both took their marriage vows seriously and were loyal to one another above all else. Fidelity at its finest.

"I wouldn't say that I *love* love him," Zenith finally told us as she carried a large, apple-filled basket. "My knees don't go weak over him or anything. But there's nobody in this world I'd rather be with, so I guess I love him some kind of way."

Oh, the honey-sweet satisfaction of being right. It wasn't enough to cut through the bitterness of our circumstances, however.

* * *

After Adelaide, Rose, and Samson had died, We were all hollowed by grief. Every day, even the ones when the sun gently kissed the earth, We felt like We moved through a dismal fog. Our physical hunger was kept at bay by their forced, extravagant meals, but our fuel was sapped away by longing and the humdrum monotony of labor. Some of us remembered Samson's quick spark for revolution and thought about reigniting that flame. But none of us had any kindling energy to spare on such visions of grandeur. Not even Jordan.

Zenith was the only one among us who seemed able to function as a whole person. She still grieved but sadness was only one of the blue hues in her eyes. As she milled and seeded across the big farm, she would dutifully whisper to herself, "Survive to be alive and thrive. Survive to be alive and thrive. Survive to be alive and thrive." We struggled to internalize the phrase for ourselves but knew that We needed to. Especially for the sake of our future children who were closer than any of us could have imagined. The They made sure of that.

One night, as We all sat together in one of our cabins, even Zenith seemed particularly troubled. But it wasn't from grief. Something about the tension in her shoulders indicated a more recent concern. Jordan knew Zenith well and was quick to ask, "Zenith, are you okay? Did something happen today?"

"It's just . . ." Zenith still hesitated. "It's just that I'm worried about Tabitha. There's something wrong with her."

Zenith explained how Tabitha had walked up to her in the orchards that afternoon. With tears pooling in her eyes and overflowing onto her cheeks, Tabitha profusely expressed her deepest condolences for the deaths of Adelaide, Rose, and Samson. Tabitha then described how much she admired each of them and wondered aloud how hard it must be to watch death swallow the people one cares about. Eventually, Tabitha got so emotional, she sobbed and shook. Tabitha leaned into Zenith's chest and Zenith held Tabitha up, just as Rose had held up Zenith so long ago.

"So, Tabitha has the capacity to sympathize," Jordan retorted. "Isn't that a good thing? Why are you worried about that?"

"But that wasn't the worrying part," Zenith persisted. "Nothing startling happened until after Tabitha stopped crying. When she pulled her face away from my chest, her cheeks were . . ."

"They were what?"

"Rusted. Tabitha's cheeks had thin trails of rust creeping down behind her drying tears."

"What?" Jordan's jaw dropped. We were all shocked. Who on this Great Famine–stricken earth could have possibly expected that?

"Exactly."

Zenith explained how it took everything in her not to gasp when she saw Tabitha's face. She stifled it because she didn't want Tabitha to feel self-conscious about opening up to her. But Zenith was worried about Tabitha because rusted cheeks were not normal. Something must have been wrong with Tabitha. Really wrong.

We all whispered among ourselves. *Maybe Tabitha was sick? Maybe the rust-like trails on her face were just dirt? Maybe Zenith mistook what she saw?*

"No," Zenith maintained, "I know what I saw. The only explanation I have, as outlandish as it sounds, is this. Tabitha and the rest of them have skin that not only *looks* metallic but actually *is* metallic. We haven't seen that until now because this is the first time any of us has seen one of them cry. Or sweat for that matter."

Though We were all still confused and concerned, We decided it would be best not to ask any questions. Lord knows what They would do to us if We did. After all, They kept their promise to feed us.

* * *

After what felt like many moons later, Zenith suddenly felt a little ill. It soon became difficult for her to walk for too long without feeling dizzy. But whenever We tried to ask how We could help her, she said she was fine. Jordan really wanted to get Zenith medicine but she insisted against it. She only agreed after she saw that Jordan was getting a little ill himself. Jordan quickly garnered up the courage to ask the soulless ones for some medicine.

"And They did me one better," he exclaimed with a toothy grin. "They gave me this stuff They call an elixir for good health, like a cure-all type of thing. They only gave me a small amount of the golden liquid, so I gave it all to Zenith this afternoon, because she's been feeling really faint over the past few days. I'll wait it out a week or so before I ask for some more."

Like Rose, Zenith died in her sleep that night. Death stole the hopeful multiplicity of blues from Zenith's eyes. Like Samson, the next morning, Jordan was paralyzed by grief. He sat motionless near Zenith's body until They came to carry it away.

"Survive to be alive and thrive," he whispered over and over again to himself.

We tried to whisper it along with him in solidarity. But by that time, all the hope within that phrase had left with Zenith's soul.

WE

We wish We could say that the longer We stayed on the big farm, the more We noticed that They constantly contradicted themselves. Unfortunately, that wasn't the case. Time and revelation aren't directly correlated. Sometimes, the truth washes over you all at once and you find yourself fighting tears of rage and confusion, wondering how on earth you managed to be so oblivious. But let's not get ahead of ourselves here. To be honest, We never saw anything clearly while We were among them. Our vision was always distorted. The initial haze of hunger was replaced by the dense fog of grief, stingy smoke of anger, and cool mist of resolve.

But even with our altered scope, We were able to notice and question some of the They's inconsistencies. For example, They claimed to be dedicated to progress and production. They said development required discomfort and sacrifice. But it seemed that We were the only ones on the big farm that produced or sacrificed anything. None of them worked alongside us in the stables, fields, or kitchen. We had only ever seen Tabitha with her legs ritually tied to a chair during dinner. They were the laziest people any of us had ever met, only seeming to exert energy when it came to overseeing our labor and attending to their sacred matters. They worshipped something called Fullness but They were never satisfied, always demanding more from us as if They were the ones who were hungry. They lived in excess but They operated out of scarcity, paranoid of the concept of waste. Surely They weren't always this way. They must have worked the land before They found us. Otherwise, the big farm could not have been the burgeoning enterprise it was upon our arrival. It couldn't have all just come out of nowhere, right?

When They weren't obsessing over maximizing production, They were talking about optimizing our reproduction. For some reason, They didn't seem to be particularly interested in reproducing among themselves. We never saw any children or babies among them. Granted, We didn't allow ourselves to think about the They procreating for long. Even now, the notion is still cringeworthy.

However, They didn't just want us to be reproducing at random. That, of course, would have been considered a waste of energy and resources. So instead, We often overheard them strategizing about which of us would be the best pairings to produce the most viable offspring. Unsurprisingly, the first of these pairs was Rose and Samson. With Samson's strength, Rose's sharp mind, and both of their striking physiques, surely their children would have been valuable. The They's ambitions were shattered by the discovery of Rose's barrenness and Samson's death. When They lost both of those "fleshed assets," much to their chagrin, They must have decided that the next best pairing was Zenith and Jordan. This time around, failure was not an option.

So, one evening, not too long after Samson passed away, We sat around the golden dinner table. The meal was just as elaborate as always. Piles and piles of charred and peppered meats. Plates and plates of different well-steamed root vegetables. Platters and platters of exotic seafood. Plenty of nuts, dried fruit, and cakes for dessert.

But the dining room air pulsed with spiked tension. Usually, after the rope tiers finished their task, They left, ensuring our legs were completely secured to the chairs. However, this time, the rope tiers stood along the walls and watched us. We had to eat under the stiff weight of their gaze. Tabitha was also in the room, standing next to the rope tiers. This wasn't too surprising. Tabitha had stopped being tied to the chairs for quite a while by that point. She had not sat with us since the night Rose was poisoned.

When We finished eating every morsel on our plates, the rope tiers freed all of the males among us from the chairs. They then ordered the men to stand behind their chairs around the golden dining room table. The women stayed tied. Startled and confused, Zenith looked over to Tabitha and asked, with her voice quivering, "Why are we not being released?"

Tabitha coyly smiled and reassured her. "Oh, my parents have a special treat for all the women. They say that it will be very good for you." Tabitha scurried out of the room.

Suddenly, a few of their young women emerged from the kitchen and placed huge carved blocks of a thick golden wax onto the plates in front of the females among us.

A rope tier, perhaps the sternest and ugliest one, stepped forward and growled, "You will not be released from the chairs until you consume every last bit of this nutrient. Let nothing go to waste."

Zenith and the rest of us women dutifully ate the chewy and viscous golden substance. It tasted sweet, almost honey-like. It wasn't unpleasant but it certainly wasn't pleasant. As We swallowed, We could feel the wax pressing into our stomachs, thickening our sides. We had never felt so full before. Our men observed the scene, paralyzed by concern and fear.

Their young women handed the rope tiers sleek silver vials with long, thin needles protruding from them. The harshest rope tier barked, "Do not squirm or you all will be tied to the chairs for the rest of the night." They held each of us down and jammed the long needles into our arms.

It felt like angry swarms of hornets were coursing through our bloodstream as the silver serum seeped into us like liquid fire.

"This is a fertility elixir," another one of the rope tiers said. "By the might of Fullness, in the name of the Embers, the elixir will prepare you all to become more useful to us. Do not be a waste."

From that evening onward, the women among us fell into the new routine of eating our meals, remaining tied to the chairs, and being injected with the stinging fertility serum.

And none of us expected that it would actually work.

* * *

We often forget exactly when the first cabin inspection happened. When We try to reach into the recesses of our memory, certain things tend to slide around. We know that it was after We had lost Samson, Rose, and Adelaide, but We don't know its place in the grand scheme of events on the big farm. But We do think it must have been after Zenith's strange encounter with Tabitha, the one when trails of rust formed on Tabitha's cheeks.

One evening, when the women among us were particularly weary from that night's fertility serum injection, We heard the bellowing voices call out to us as They approached our cabins. "Cabin inspection, cabin inspection, cabin inspection!" They kept chanting.

They swung our wooden cabin doors open so hard that the doors ricocheted off the walls with loud, sharp cracks and nearly broke. We almost jumped out of our skin but We were able to remain stone still as They paced through our cabins. For all of the pomp and circumstance, They didn't look around seriously. They just walked through each of the four cabins a couple times and quickly glanced over everything in plain sight. Further evidence of their exemplary laziness.

One of the They leaders warned, "If we find what we are looking for, curses in the name of the Embers will fall upon you and your future generations. You are not worthy of the sacred knowledge of Fullness. It goes against your flesh."

JORDAN

We finally let ourselves rest when the moon reached its cool peak in the sky. After eating some roasted insects, most of us slept soundly as We huddled together for community and warmth. But some of us were wide awake through the night, contemplating the journey ahead of us. Soon "escape" wouldn't suffice in achieving our ultimate goals. We all know We need to have a more certain idea of what We want the future to hold but some of us are more preoccupied with these considerations than others. Of the beloved ones We lost, Rose and Samson would have tossed and turned, feverishly plotting out our next steps in their minds. Adelaide and Zenith would have been concerned about the logistics of food and shelter but they also would not have let their worries keep them from sleeping and dreaming. And Jordan would have begun to snore as soon as he closed his eyes. Jordan wasn't one to think much about the future. His keen eyes never bothered to look beyond the present.

"Tomorrow isn't promised to anyone, you know," he'd say, studying the water-pruned grooves in his hands. "Besides, there's too much to do and see today."

Even now, it is painful to soak in the reality of those words.

By God's grace, tomorrow did come for all of us that still remain. We rose before the sun, stirring awake when the sky first blushed at dawn. We collected some morning dew to drink and then started our day of running. We let the wind carry our strides until We made it to another river. Now, We are resting on the bank. The river water is cool, dark, and too deep to wade through. Most of us are going to have to swim across, carrying the weaker swimmers on our backs.

We can all swim at least a little bit but this is not the time to take risks in testing ability. Praise God the currents don't look too strong.

* * *

Jordan knew a thing or two about currents. He knew a lot about the movement of water, from rivers carving themselves toward the sea to mischievous ocean waves trying to disobey the tides. Like Zenith, Jordan was an island dweller before the apocalyptic Great Famine. In fact, there is a lot of overlap between Zenith and Jordan's respective origins. Their pasts were braided together in ways that were never fully revealed to us but everything We learned about Jordan's home island, We learned from Zenith after persistent questioning. According to Zenith, Jordan's island was a lot like hers, except for one main difference. Instead of a high mountain, the characteristic landmark of Jordan's island was a powerful, rageful river that often flooded. That's all We ever really found out but even that wouldn't be until later.

When We first met Jordan further along the coastal beach, he didn't mention how he'd gotten there. He just boldly walked up and asked if he could join us while We looked for food. We said yes and he became one of us. Simple. We didn't ask him further questions then. We saw the broken planks of wood washed ashore that looked like they were once fashioned into a makeshift raft. We made some inferences from that but We definitely wanted to know more. Jordan's long, gaunt frame was covered in stubborn seaweed. His skin was a deep brown with an ocean-blue undertone. His short hair and narrow eyebrows were one shade lighter than night-sky black. But most notably, his gaze was a piercing silver. Gazes have color and looking Jordan in the eye was enough to convince anyone of that. And though We wanted to ask questions about his past, something about the sharpened silver of his gaze asserted that Jordan wasn't one for reminiscing.

Jordan was a man of impulse. He was always in the midst of the action. If there were fruits to be sliced, fish to be caught, game to be hunted, kindling to be gathered, or insects to be roasted, Jordan would do anything and everything before sitting still. And even when he did sit still, he would only do it if he were engaged in lively conversation, often with Samson or Zenith.

One night, about a half-moon before the deception, Jordan and Samson were roasting fish Jordan had caught over a fire Samson had started. They whispered because they thought the rest of us were asleep.

With his eyes fixed on the heart of the fire, Samson asked Jordan when he was going to tell Zenith how he felt. Jordan really needed to take his own advice.

Jordan sighed. "Oh, Samson. Poor confused Samson. I don't like Zenith that way. Zenith and I are just friends."

Samson laughed softly. "Don't try to deny looking into Zenith's eyes. We've all seen you do it, you know."

"Well, who can blame me?" Jordan protested. "The blues in Zenith's irises are magnetic. I've tried counting all the different shades and I've gotten to fourteen so far. Fourteen is the number I get to before I start to panic about Zenith catching me counting. If she knew I did it, she'd think I'm crazy."

After a long, silent period of listening to the crackling flames, Jordan finally sighed again. "You want the whole truth, Samson?"

"I'm ready to hear it, when you're ready to tell it."

"Well, I think I'm drawn to Zenith because she reminds me of the parts of myself I've lost since the start of the Great Famine. Growing up, my favorite color was blue. I loved the blues of the river, ocean, and sky. I even liked the blue in the hottest part of the fire. But when the Great Famine hit and I entered survival mode, I forgot I had a favorite color. I forgot I had a favorite anything. But I remembered blue and all its shades when I really looked into Zenith's eyes for the first time. It was like the part of me I thought I'd lost had been found in her."

Samson nodded thoughtfully, processing the gravitas of Jordan's confession. He insisted that sounded like love to him but he promised to try to respect what Jordan said about his own feelings.

Samson and Jordan took the charred black fish out of the fire and ate them dutifully. As usual, they laughed until sleep overtook them.

* * *

Back when the soulless ones first brought us to their land, perhaps about three days after our first meal there, They had all of us go to the riverbank and strip naked. And then, one by one, They pushed us into the frigid water. They sternly instructed us to swim to the other bank and back. Then, They retreated and stood a safe distance from the bank. They made sure that none of us drowned. That would have been a wasteful disposal of their new property. We know that now in hindsight. But They watched as most of us flailed and trembled and choked and fought tears of panic.

It wasn't the swimming itself that was the issue. We could all swim at least a little bit and the river currents were weak. It was the cruel, chilling shock of the water. It was being naked and watched. It was processing the reality of being pushed in. It was knowing an elusive *something* wasn't quite right about this from the metallic taste in our mouths. Jordan didn't seem to mind the situation though. He was merely in his second home. We used to wonder if he had developed gills. In the same way that Samson took command over fire, Jordan coalesced with the water. He didn't just swim. He flew, glided, and danced through the river, showing off every kind of stroke he knew.

When We were all out of the river, passing their ridiculous test, They gave us ragged towels to dry ourselves off. One of them, a stout bald man with an unkempt beard, shouted over to Jordan, "You're a good swimmer, boy. A mighty good swimmer. We sure could use you around here."

They made Jordan a fisherman's boy, someone who oversees the catch and dives to untangle fishing nets if necessary. And it was necessary on a daily basis. Of all of us, Jordan was the one who was covered with the most cuts and bruises at any given time. The rope burns on his legs were often joined by small scrapes from the fishing nets and river debris. His hands were also occasionally covered in cuts from poor knife handling while slicing open the caught fish. But again, Jordan did not mind the situation. He didn't think too much about it, just lived through it like he always did, localized in the present. He almost enjoyed his assigned occupation.

"I like being in the water and handling the fish," he'd tell us, shaking water out of his ears, "but I'd rather be doing a lot of other things in the water, like going for a swim. You know what I mean?"

The only one of us that really understood what he meant was Zenith and We watched as the quiet connection between them strengthened.

"I don't know exactly how I feel about Zenith anymore," Jordan finally said, "but I know that she's like the color blue to me, and that's all I need to make sense of right now."

* * *

If whatever pulsed between Jordan and Zenith couldn't be called love, it was definitely loyalty. In rare, still moments, We could always count on seeing the two of them together, exchanging deep knowing glances that only they understood. They always sat either next to or directly across from each other in the big dining room. They were the first to study and nurse each other's rope burns. And who can forget their secret swims at night in the river?

Tabitha seemed to be the only one on the big farm who couldn't see the signs of Jordan and Zenith's close bond. Or perhaps she chose to ignore them. For even from the first time Tabitha sat at the dining table with us, We noticed how her eyes carefully traced Jordan's jawline as he chewed. Early on, We assumed it was solely out of an innocent curiosity. Jordan probably wasn't the most stunning out of all of us. That superlative would more aptly suit Rose or Samson. But it could be argued that Jordan was the most interesting one among us. Something about his silver gaze was always so captivating. And besides, though We were never sure how old Tabitha was, We guessed she was about the same age as Adelaide. No longer a child, not quite a woman, and too young to be concerned with romance.

Or so We thought.

One evening, after a particularly elaborate dinner, Jordan burst through one of our cabin doors as it swung back with a loud crack. He pulled up a wooden chair and sat down abruptly, only to stand again to begin pacing. We asked Jordan what was wrong but he insisted that he needed to know that Zenith was out of the cabin before he could explain anything further.

Jordan wanting Zenith's absence? That was certainly a first. When We assured him that Zenith was in the big house washing dishes with Rose, Jordan seemed less worried, but his apparent anger intensified.

"The audacity of that girl!" he fumed. "The sheer audacity!"

Who on earth was he talking about? Zenith?

"No, not Zenith. Tabitha! I'm telling you; she's got some nerve."

Jordan described how earlier that afternoon, Tabitha had approached him while he was walking from the riverbank to the big house. From what he could tell, no one else was around. Tabitha seemed to know that for certain from the way she unabashedly looked at Jordan. And her gaze wasn't one of innocent curiosity.

Jordan huffed. "She started saying crazy things like she likes 'my sleek skin-and-bones body.' She's confused, isn't she? She can't be saying nonsense like that. It's not becoming. No ma'am, it's not. What kind of man wants to be told he's skinny? She won't be getting any attention with any of those so-called compliments."

We wanted to tell Jordan that the fact he was called skinny was far from the most disconcerting part of the interaction he depicted. But then, Jordan went on to explain something even more unsettling.

"It gets worse," he groaned, and he pulled something out of his almost-tattered back pocket. It was a small, black leather-bound book with the word *Full* engraved on the front cover. The book was beautiful in a simple way. As We passed it around, We realized it was the first book any of us had seen in a long time. None of us had noticed any books in or around the big house before. Where did Tabitha get this book? Why did she give it to Jordan?

"I don't know." A new wave of frustration washed over Jordan. "Don't ask me to make sense of Tabitha's nonsense. She wanted me to promise her that I'd read it. But I didn't say a word. Just stared at her blankly until she could take a hint. I didn't have anything nice to say, so I said nothing. I don't want to read that book though."

We insisted that he didn't have to read it, but with a title like *Full*, We were naturally intrigued. All of us convinced Jordan that it would be best to keep the book somewhere in our cabins and revisit it later. Jordan shoved the *Full* book deep into the straw of his bed, which is where it remained hidden for a long time. We advised Jordan to handle the situation with Tabitha delicately going forward.

From that point onward, when We all sat at the big dining room table, Jordan avoided eye contact with Tabitha at all costs. Per our guidance, he was subtle about it, so those who were unaware of the matter would not have suspected anything. Zenith was completely oblivious and Jordan wanted it to stay that way. We agreed that would be for the best and never told her anything. But even now, We wonder how much They knew about Tabitha's advances. Could that have been one of the reasons They demanded Jordan and Zenith get married? Perhaps that question, among many others, will forever remain unanswered.

* * *

Jordan handled grief differently from the rest of us. He was a man of action, so he coped through movement. When We lost Adelaide, while the rest of us woke up crying at dawn, Jordan would leave the cabins early to get ahead on his work on the river. At first, We thought this was cold and distant of him. We knew that he and Adelaide weren't exactly close but he could at least shed a tear or mourn in some other, more recognizable way. But then We realized that whenever one of us said Adelaide's name, We could see a wave of pain swell up in Jordan's eyes. He also talked a lot less. He no longer engaged in lively discussions with anyone other than Samson or Zenith.

After Rose died, Jordan only spoke to Zenith, when he was spoken to, and in vain efforts to console Samson. Zenith came to miss the once vibrant round timbre of her husband's voice but she knew not to mention anything about this to him. Jordan would have just fallen more silent out of shame of disappointing her. It doesn't have to make sense to be true. That's just how Jordan was.

When Samson died, Jordan left the room whenever one of us said Samson's name. He couldn't take it. Jordan spent as much time on the river as he could, only going to the big house when ordered to for meals, and only coming back to the cabins to sleep next to Zenith.

And when Zenith died . . . Oh Lord have mercy . . . When Zenith died . . .

Jordan's silver gaze dulled and he completely stopped talking to everyone. He just mumbled to himself. He refused to be still. Jordan had lost a piece of himself and transformed into motion. In his eyes, he had become motion without purpose. For Jordan, there was no spark of revolution, nothing beyond his bereft present. We tried to comfort him without success. The "survive to be alive and thrive" phrase barely helped. Jordan's soul followed Zenith to heaven. In his final days, his body often collapsed into sleep against his will. But even in sleep he was restless, tossing and turning throughout the night.

Every once in a while, We'd hear him mutter, "Race you to the other side of the river, Zenith." That really broke our hearts.

Ten days after Zenith's death, Jordan was a dead man walking. More than that. A fleshed apparition. The They had noticed Jordan had fallen ill and tried to give him a *real* cure-all that dawn. Surely, They didn't want to lose their best swimmer and fisherman. Jordan put the cool gray liquid in his mouth and stored it in his cheeks until the They left the room. As soon as the door closed behind them, he spit out the medicine all over his bed mattress. We don't blame him for this, of course. He had every reason to be suspicious of them.

"I'm not sleeping here tonight anyway," Jordan grumbled, looking at the splattered mess. "I'm going to swim up the river to find a way out of this place."

They found Jordan's body washed up on the riverbank later that evening. Tabitha was the one who gave us the news. The man that seemed to be part fish swallowed too much water and drowned. Improbable, but not impossible. Not impossible for a body without a soul.

It wasn't until after Jordan's death that We finally considered running from their big farm. Could being fed really be worth all this pain? Could it?

WE

In all the time that We were with the They, We almost never saw them leave the big farm. Early on, We thought it was a bit strange. Why would They have four golden carriages, or even more, housed in the stables and never use them? Well, now We know that was probably another sign of the excess They'd acquired. And as We think about it now, it makes sense that They hardly ever left. They had no reason to. Everything that They needed was either already somewhere on the big farm or brought to them by their visitors. We can only remember seeing them go beyond the big farm's borders of oasis once.

It was early dawn. Naturally, We were already awake, preparing ourselves for another draining work day. As We filed out of our cabins and walked toward the big house for breakfast, We saw about twenty They men walking in the distance over the edge of the big farm's property. Not coolly lounging in a polished golden carriage while surveying their surroundings. They didn't take any of their carriages. Not riding toward the horizon on any of their many majestic stallions. They didn't take any of their horses. Given all the options the men had, We thought their choice of transportation was bizarre.

Why are those They men just walking? Where on earth are They going?

At first, We thought that maybe they were going to see their visitors. They might have been curious about their guests' established oasis. They may have wanted to determine whether it was even remotely comparable to what They had developed. They were conceited and insecure that way. But then again, We figured that if They were heading toward their visitors, the They men might have put in a little bit more effort to be impressive. They definitely would have put on airs and been more likely to use their fancy carriages. They love a good enviable spectacle. With this line of reasoning, We ruled out their guests' home as a possibility for their destination. We were thrust into the throng of our daily duties before We could think about it any further.

The They men returned right at dusk just before dinner, carrying five of the largest baskets any of us had ever seen up the path toward the big house. It took four men to pick up just one of the baskets, and even then, the lifters struggled under the weight. A few of us saw their knees buckling and approached to help but the carriers barked in disgust, "Away from the baskets, fleshed ones. Do not defile the sacred."

None of us knew what was inside these holy baskets as their contents were concealed by tightly woven lids.

Once the They men reached the front of the big house, the lead carrier triumphantly called, "Brothers and sisters! My fellow victors! Tonight, we claim Fullness through sacrifice! Greater reward comes at a greater price!"

Suddenly, the rest of the They streamed out of the big house, giddily chanting, "Sacrifice! Sacrifice! Fullness and sacrifice!" Though it rarely ever happened, the They were once again in good spirits. And it was absolutely horrifying.

To the growing crowd's delight, the carriers dropped the huge baskets with a loud thud and pulled off the lids to reveal the offerings for the ceremony. Each basket held two of the same type of dark, gangly creature We had seen them slaughter in the wilderness. There were ten squirming, poor, wide-eyed animals in total, bound by rope around their legs. Though the beasts tried to move, We could tell that they had more or less resigned themselves to their tragic fate.

The men killed the offering animals like They did in the wilderness. They grabbed and tore off each of the beasts' limbs while they were still alive. However, instead of collecting their lifeblood in smooth black jars, They threw the dismembered carcasses back into the baskets and carried them into the big house as quickly as They could. In their haste, the baskets leaked a trail of dark crimson blood. We assume They then tossed the twisted flesh mounds into the furnace flame. We could smell the putrid stench of burning blood, muscle, and fur. The rest of the They cheered, caught up in some frenzied revelry. Tabitha was somewhere among them, no doubt. Once They calmed down, their metallic faces hardened and They ordered us to scrub the drying trail of blood from the wooden floors. It took everything in our power not to vomit or faint.

When it was time for dinner, none of us had much of an appetite. As They forced us to sit in the chairs, it was hard for us to think about consuming flesh after knowing innocent creatures had been thrown into a greedy furnace. As We itched and writhed under the familiar sting of rope burn, the lead rope tier declared, "Fleshed ones, we need you now more than ever." He leaned down and grabbed the rope around one of our young women's legs. He pulled and pulled on it until the young woman could not help but squeal in pain. He smiled and continued to say, "Fleshed ones, we need you now more than ever. By the might of the Embers, Fullness will finally be ours. And it's all because of you."

TABITHA?

All of us have made it across the river. The currents were stronger than any of us had anticipated. We struggled through the swirling, deep waters. Now, most of our energy is left dragging the sediment at the bottom of the river.

It is dusk again and We have decided to stay on the riverbank through the night. It is not too cold, so We are thankful for the wind drying our water-pruned skin. The ground We are resting on is still damp. Most of us are lying on our backs, gazing up at the sky. We watch as the warm twilight colors recede to night black with all its stars. Some of us are going to slip into sleep soon. But most of us will probably keep vigil until dawn. Our bodies may be exhausted but our spirits are awake, stirring. We are praying for a greater sense of direction.

In the time before the Great Famine, each of us used to dread crossroads. Knowing that one turn could change someone's path, or even destination, was often daunting. We had a lingering fear of the wrong turn. But now, We wish for two roads diverging in a golden wood. There are no crossroads, and no clear turns or choices, in the ruined wilderness. And as far as We know, We can go any way but backward. We need to decide what to think and where to go next.

And yet, it is still difficult for us to focus on our future when so much of our past remains unresolved. Perhaps most notably, We don't know what to think of Tabitha. How should We frame her in our history? It isn't simple. This is a different kind of crossroads. Was she our enemy? Was she our friend? Was she a double agent? Was she a tragic victim? We cannot reach a consensus on who she was or how she fits into the fabric of who We have become. To be clear, Tabitha is not one of us. But she is also not one of them. She is lost somewhere in the miserable fog of not being part of anything. In the whirl of her confusion, We do not know which of her choices We should accredit to her. She hurt us deeply and was far from a saint. Even if she were to die for us now, We still wouldn't consider her a martyr. But wouldn't it be wrong not to acknowledge some of Tabitha's kindness and goodwill? Wouldn't excluding the risk she took leave a gaping hole in our story?

Maybe it is best to recognize how Tabitha helped us. We still keep the letter she wrote us, alternating who holds or keeps it in their back pocket as We run. We even kept it safe and dry when We crossed rivers. Not for Tabitha's sake but for ours. When her name is spoken on the lips of our children, may it always be tinged with ambivalence.

* * *

It was a cold night about a moon after Jordan died. We were all inside the first of the four cabins in our living row. We had not seen Tabitha since the day that They had found Jordan's body. Again, it seemed that she was no longer required to sit with us at the big table. We noticed her absence but didn't think much of it. Perhaps it was for the best. So, We were startled when We heard her usually timid voice shout, "Cabin inspection!" as she burst through the wooden door.

Tabitha was alone and quickly closed the door behind her. Her glistening, metallic face was stiff but not stern. We could hear her joints creak as she walked across the dirt floors. She glanced around the main room quickly, not really inspecting much of anything. Their laziness had seeped into her too.

Suddenly, Tabitha stopped walking and recoiled under our gaze. She quickly pulled out a folded piece of paper from her back pocket and handed it over to one of us, whispering, "Promise me you'll read this. I can't stay here while you do it but promise me all of you will read this."

We all heard her, so We all nodded, watching in solemn awe as a single streak of rust followed a tear down Tabitha's face. Zenith had been right in what she saw all along.

Tabitha, stifling the urge to cry, left the cabin, closing the wooden door behind her. Dismayed, We gathered around in a circle and took turns whispering parts of Tabitha's letter aloud.

First of all, We noticed that she addressed us as the "We People." That unexpectedly touched our hearts. We had only heard any of the They call us the "fleshed ones," which made our skin crawl. Secondly, We noticed that Tabitha had written the letter in *our* language to the best of her ability. She would borrow a Common Tongue word whenever she seemed to forget our vocabulary, but on the whole, she articulated herself well. We weren't sure how to feel about that. On the one hand, it meant that she was listening to us, perhaps with the desire to truly know us. But on the other hand, Tabitha was *listening* to us, undermining the one measure of privacy We tried to maintain. This was just the root of our ambivalence.

Tabitha was really nervous about writing this letter. And We knew she had every reason to be. She was putting herself in potential danger and We could see the jitters in her handwriting. Worried about what We would think of her, she rambled a bit before getting to the heart of the matter. Tabitha had some confessions to make. She promised to share with us as much of the truth as possible, everything she knew.

Tabitha was not the naive, lovestruck, confused young lady We thought she was. All of her seemingly genuine interactions with us were underpinned by mixed motives. Her parents and the rest of the They ordered her to observe our behaviors during dinner and report her findings back to them. She was supposed to objectively examine us as if We were just caged animals. And if she did well, she would finally be approved to enter the next phase with everyone else. *What on earth was a phase?* As if anticipating our question, she wrote that she'd explain what a "phase" was later in the letter. As much as We wanted to deny it, Tabitha knew us well.

She tried to monitor us coldly but that went against something in her nature. She expressed how much she came to like us. She even wrote, "Proximity became affection, one could say," which softened our hearts against our will again. We rolled our eyes when she mentioned that she cried when Adelaide died. We didn't need her pity. We cringed as she described how infatuated she was with Jordan. She even risked it all and gave him a *Full* book so that he could become part of her family. Maybe she needed our pity. But her next confession made our stomachs drop and blood boil. Apparently, her parents ordered her to hurt one of us to prove her loyalty to the They.

Tabitha was the one who poisoned Rose.

It didn't matter that Tabitha didn't mean to kill Rose. She insisted that she just wanted to make Rose sick by putting a little bit of poison in her cream puff. She then accused her parents of catching onto her plan and putting a more concentrated solution of the poison in the vial. She even swore a part of her died with Rose. How on earth could she even fathom making excuses for herself? Who cared about intentions when the impact was literally deadly? And to add insult to injury, she feigned an apology and unloaded even more devastating information in one fell swoop:

I know you all must hate me now. I would hate me now too if I were you. But I want to somehow do something to show you that I am not like my family. That I wish I could be more like you. Losing Adelaide, Rose, Samson, Zenith, and Jordan, especially Jordan, was absolutely devastating. And watching my family feed all their dead bodies to the Full furnace flame broke my heart, especially after finding out Zenith was pregnant. But to move into the next phase with my family, my heart isn't allowed to be breakable. Soon, I won't even have a heart to break.

She then hurriedly scribbled that We were part of Phase Three, whatever on God's earth that was, and that her parents got the *Full* books from a wise figure wearing a dark, hooded cloak in the desert like it wasn't important.

Too shocked to allow the full gravitas of our emotions to wash over us, We quickly dug the *Full* book out of the straw in what was once Jordan's bed, its black leather cover worn and dirty from being hidden. Outraged, dismayed, and curious, We opened the book to the first page. The book's complete title was wildly disconcerting:

Full: Your New Furnace and the Flame Beyond Humanity.

But We were even more livid as the Table of Contents seared itself into our collective memory:

Introduction: Welcome to Your New Full Furnace

Phase One: Installation and Flame Spark

Phase Two: Satiation and Infrastructural Development
Phase Three: Liberation from Flesh through Subjugation of Fleshed Others
Phase Four: Propagation of Fuel for Flame Autonomy Stabilization
Phase Five: Extraction of Metallized Organs with Flame as Ultimate Fuel
Conclusion: Fullness Beyond Humanity

Words fail to describe the searing pain and anger We felt then. How *dare* she? How dare They? The sheer audacity! The sheer evil! It took everything in us not to rip down everything surrounding us in a righteous, avenging rage. The They would need jars and jars of Adelaide's healing salve by the time We were through with them. We wished We had and could wield a dagger like Rose. We longed for Samson's strength to break apart the cabin walls. If only Zenith were there with her gentle wisdom. If only Jordan were there to anchor and amuse us with his quick wit. God's angels had to hold us back from drawing weapons. But when the calmness of clarity descended on us, We decided We would read the rest of the *Full* book before doing anything too rash. We would finally discover what They believed. What They wanted from us.

And what We needed to do to escape them.

WE

We read the *Full* book feverishly, in silence and in whispers.
We strained our eyes to see the small print in the moonlight
as the They slept. We had no idea how much the book had
dictated the thoughts and actions of the They but We were
desperate to discover their true motivations. We devoured
this book over the course of seven nights, one for each book
section. And We came to discover that the roles of victims
and perpetrators were much more complicated than any one
of us could ever have anticipated.

The introduction was eerie, not just in its substance, but
also in its form. Though the table of contents had clearly
been written in Common Tongue, the true text of the book
shape-shifted. As We each took turns glancing over the pages,
the letters twisted into the scripts of our respective native
languages. In hindsight, We figure the *Full* book's morphing
ability is meant to appeal to its reader's sense of self. But then,
We were too desperate to be astonished or amazed. We were
just all the more careful in guarding our hearts.

Whoever wrote this book seemed to almost *know* that the
Great Famine would come. As if it were a preordained era.
Apparently, the Full furnaces were strongest during times
of heightened resource scarcity but hunger is ever present.
Even in abundance, there's always need. Always a chance for
growth or restoration. Readers were encouraged to think of
constantly wanting more as a valuable manifestation of ambi-
tion, not a form of greed. The eradication of lacking would
ultimately blaze the trail to ever-emerging progress. Real life
could only start through escaping the flesh. The Full flame
was the destined end of pain and hunger and the promised

beginning of a satisfied humanity and a brighter future. And rather ominously, the introduction was by a group that called themselves the Embers. Perhaps one of the Embers was the figure in the dark, hooded cloak that Tabitha mentioned in her letter. Perhaps another one of the Embers was the figure Adelaide and April encountered in the woods.

The next night, We read about Phase One. According to the *Full* book, the They must have found the barest part of the wilderness in order for the Full flame to have the opportunity to display the complete glory of its powers. After following complex instructions to build the furnace itself, the They had to stock the flame's base fuel of wood, leaves, and drained mitis blood. Mitis must have been the name of the gentle slain beasts that We saw in the wilderness and on the big farm. At least one of these mitis creatures was sacrificed at the outset of each phase to ensure a submissive and well-oriented heart in the midst of the process. Then, all They needed to do was simply incant, "May Fullness burn within you," to make the first flame leap from the desperate heat of the air.

The following night, our stomachs turned as We read about Phase Two. During this stage, the Full spark developed into a thin flame with its own distinct color. As the Full flame grew, it shaped itself to articulate its demands for specific types of fuel. And of course, the fuel had to be attained at all costs. In return for utter obedience, the young Full flame used its power to create a land of abundance for the They, its worshippers, generating ample food. Also, any metal tool forged in the Full flame itself would be imbued with its dark power and shine the same fiery shade. Just like the violet key that Adelaide swallowed.

But all of this could only manifest under one crucial condition: All the food the Full flame provided could not go to waste. Every morsel that was not consecrated for the Full flame had to be consumed. Absolutely *nothing* could go to waste and the flame would not take unholy leftovers. Though the They's hunger was satiated, They had only one way to ensure that it would never return—escaping the depraved prison of their flesh.

We were particularly nervous as We turned through the Phase Three chapter because We knew this was when We entered the They's twisted tale. We were the ones burdened with the work of maintaining the growing big farm so the They could focus on feeding the Full flame what it desired. While We were there, They transferred their flesh onto us by some process that We couldn't comprehend through nebulous words. The book instructed the They to feed us, the fleshed ones, well as a testament to the Full flame's provision and might. We as the fleshed ones were especially not allowed to waste or be wasted. The *Full* book specifically mentioned that if any one of the fleshed ones died, our bodies were to be fed to the Full flame. And if these steps were executed correctly, the They's bodies would become increasingly metallized and less dependent on food, solely craving the presence of the Full flame itself.

As We carefully read Phase Four, We understood the utilizable importance of the They's relationship with their visitors. According to the book, the more fleshed ones there were, the better, for the sake of sustainability and the Full flame's well-being. The *Full* book commanded that the They obtained a fertility enhancer in any form at all costs, even if it would be through trade. This explained why They were willing to work with their visitors, whom They could barely tolerate. They were willing to do anything as long as They were able to get this critical piece to ascend to the next phase.

Phase Five had gruesome depictions of proper metallized organ extraction methods. They pained us as We read them. But We also knew that the They would no longer have flesh by that stage. Allegedly, They'd no longer feel pain or anything by then, which to us, seemed to be an even more tragic fate. Upon the removal of the organs, the Full flame would reverently be transferred from the furnace to burn in the spaces where the They's hearts once were. The Full flame would be the They's source of life and direction for generations to come.

And finally, as We read the startling conclusion, We realized the They and their visitors were probably not the only ones with Full flames. The Embers' final vision was for there to be Full flames in every visible color. The worthy tier of humanity would be elevated beyond their flesh and be enveloped by Fullness now and for all eternity.

We were not prepared for the weighted sadness that would descend upon our fleshed hearts when We finished the *Full* book. Our souls ached as We realized that the They could have been a We once. If They had never encountered one of the Embers, They could have still been a We. The Embers had victimized the They and their visitors like the They victimized us. If only history could be rewritten. They might have been just like us, hungry, desperate, and painfully naive. Fully acknowledging this made us hate and pity them all the more.

ISAAC

Morning is here again and the sunshine lush and golden. Some of us did in fact keep vigil until dawn but a quiet peace then soothed us, allowing everyone to sleep at least a little. We are still tired but in an almost soft way, like a gentle hush over our voices and movements. We are not weary and confused like We were last night. Today, this morning, We have a rejuvenated sense of purpose and direction. For as We wrestled through the night, We received the blessing of answered prayer.

To be clear, We still have doubts about where We are going. Our prayers were answered miraculously but not quite overtly. Sometimes, prayers are answered through visions and signs. We know that is not something that is confined to ancient days. Yet, other times, like this one, answered prayer is more subtle. We feel tenderly held by the One beyond ourselves in the light of a future hope. The warm sunshine and the chance to bask in its radiance was the answer We needed. We now know where We are meant to go.

We will run to the horizon.

We need to go to the horizon. The place holds infinite possibilities. In the same way that Rose described plants as the children of two different realms, of the earth and the sky, maybe the horizon is a place where heaven meets earth. The horizon might be like a return to the Garden of Eden, a paradise that is often elusive but not entirely lost. Perhaps the horizon is the only sacred place left in this Great Famine–stricken world. We need to go there because We know that is where We will be drawn closer to our purpose. In the space beyond limits, We will long to excel and succeed together, for the sake of ourselves and for the sake of our future generations.

Though our hearts break over what might have been, whenever We dream of our children, We see Isaac's face. Or at least the hypnotic whirl of combined features that could have been Isaac's face. We see endless chances and the promised potential to flourish in love. Isaac embodies why We move. We never want our children to endure the pain and agony of hunger. But more importantly, We also never want our children to experience the pain and agony of not being seen as human. Our children will never be reduced to their flesh, solely as a means to an end. We know our children will be much more than that. Isaac would have been so much more than that. And, to us, he still is so much more than that. For even in the tragedy of losing Isaac and his parents, Zenith and Jordan, and even the tragedy of losing our other beloved ones, We have a glimmer of an enlightened peace.

We once made a vow against hunger. We used to think that hunger was our greatest enemy. How could We not? Hunger can be cruel, merciless, and ravenous, ripping away at our insides, feasting on our bodily weakness. It thrives on perpetuated scarcity and needless disparity. And yet, though hunger can still be dreadful, it helped forge our family. We would have never become a *We* if We did not unite over a shared need. We will strive to diminish hunger among ourselves and others that We will meet on our journey to the horizon. But now We know. Now We know that hunger is not our greatest enemy. Our capacity to feel and endure hunger and lacking and pain reveals We are human.

The soulless ones are not our greatest enemies. They were as deceived as We were. Our ultimate enemy is greed. For greed hardens hearts and minds and renders other people as less than human, as merely flesh.

Our children will be more than flesh. Our children will be more than animated metal. Our children will be completely and unabashedly human.

* * *

Not long after jumping the broom, Zenith and Jordan dreamed of having children of their own. Zenith had always longed to be a mother. She wanted the chance to nurse and cherish her children's lives, helping them navigate right and wrong while still preserving innocence and wonder. Jordan, on the other hand, did not think much about fatherhood until Zenith lay next to him in bed for the first time. Some nights, We heard Zenith and Jordan in whispered debate with each other over possible baby names. They did all of their dreaming and planning discreetly, stifled by pangs of guilt. It didn't feel right for them to talk about their future children when they knew Rose and Samson could never have any of their own. Zenith and Jordan's guilt only deepened with the sorrow of losing Rose and Samson. Yet they still dreamed of and considered names, perhaps as a way to cope with their grief. Perhaps as a means to hope for a type of freedom. Zenith and Jordan decided that if they were to have a son, they would name him Isaac, a sign of covenant and new beginnings. They had not chosen a name for a daughter by the time Zenith died.

Zenith probably died just as she was beginning to feel the seed take root inside of her. That would explain her dizziness.

And even though They injected the women among us with a silver fertility serum not long after Samson's death, none of us expected it to actually work. Zenith likely didn't know she was pregnant. Jordan didn't know either. None of us found out until Tabitha told us in her letter. We shiver when we think of how They were able to determine Zenith's pregnancy. That is one of the many things We hope to never fully know about them.

As We developed our plans for escape, our hearts were filled with dreams of who Isaac might have been. We could almost see baby Isaac with Zenith's short, loose curls. When We secretly stored supplies for our exodus by night, We painted Isaac's big, beckoning, kaleidoscope eyes with flecks of silver dancing between crystalline shards of sapphire, emerald, and amber in our minds. As We examined and nursed each other's rope burns, We saw Isaac's smooth, rich, mahogany skin.

When We worked even harder around the big farm to build physical stamina for the journey ahead, We envisioned Isaac with Jordan's thin, wiry frame as he grew older. Isaac would have been quiet yet confident. Quiet like his mother and confident like his father. We didn't know what he would have liked but We knew what he would have been able to do. If he were anything like his parents, he would have been able to swim long and fast and far. Zenith and Jordan would have introduced Isaac to the water by moonlight as soon as he was old enough to crawl. Tears spilled down our cheeks whenever We imagined Isaac feeling the coolness of the river water on his skin for the first time, his kaleidoscope eyes wide with wonder.

Isaac reminded us why We had to run from the big farm. Whenever We had our doubts, A haunting question propelled us forward: How would They have treated Isaac? We didn't know but We knew We never truly wanted to find out. How would They have treated baby Isaac? Would They have tied his plump infant legs to a highchair? Would Isaac's soft skin have chafed from rope burn? Would They have fed him at all or put some rations aside for us to feed him? Would They have let Zenith leave her work duties to properly nurse Isaac? Would They have closely watched and examined him, gathering data on how he grew? At what age would They have deemed Isaac old enough to work? If Isaac wasn't what They wanted, would They have ultimately succumbed to their visitors' offer and traded him away? Somehow, he may have had even more tragic a fate than swallowing the same poison as his mother, perhaps more violent an end than being swallowed by the Full flame.

We had no young children or babies with us, much to the soulless ones' chagrin. None of us gave birth while We were among them. Everyone on the big farm also seemed to have been at least the age when adulthood was just within reach. So, We had no sense how They treated anyone who had yet to reach the age of reason. We were thankful no children were around. No child deserved to be deceived into seeing reason in the big farm's madness.

* * *

Fortunately for us, even after Tabitha wrote us that elucidating letter, the rest of the They didn't seem to suspect anything. They were so oblivious, in fact, that They officially put Tabitha in charge of the cabin inspections. We doubt They would have done that if They had known that We knew more than They thought. So, at night, We gathered loose cloth to make blankets and tried our best to discreetly pack supplies for our escape. When Tabitha came to inspect our cabins, she didn't say anything, choosing to turn a blind eye. Though our feelings toward her were still rightfully mixed, We were thankful for her then. We would often exchange weighted glances with Tabitha, trying to silently convey our plans without trusting her with all the details. But We knew she knew what We were about to do.

As We read the *Full* book, We tried to note certain critical details that would help us determine how to go about our exodus. As much as We wish We could have just escaped under the dark cloak of nightfall, it was much more complicated than that. Sure, They were lazy and probably wouldn't have stirred from their slumber to pursue us. But We still felt like We couldn't afford to leave too much up to chance. After all, We were their assets, our flesh serving as a means for them to escape theirs. Maybe They would think We were worth pursuing. We couldn't risk that. We would need some kind of diversion. A carefully crafted ruse that would make them vulnerable to their own desires. We spent tireless nights in hushed discussions about strategy and logistics until finally settling on a course of action. We were going to flee from the big farm. And Tabitha was going to help us.

One night, as Tabitha was doing yet another cabin inspection, We handed her a note that outlined her role in our escape. If Tabitha really meant what she said by wanting to help us, We had devised a plan that would help benefit us, her, and the rest of the They. Here was what she needed to do:

While the rest of the They were sleeping, Tabitha would have to sneak into the room housing the blazing furnace. A small part of us felt guilty for sending her into the belly of the beast alone, but really, she'd brought most of this upon herself. All of them had. Besides, she would surely have better luck entering the Full flame's presence than any of us did. We did not know whether the flame possessed any profound sense of intellect or was solely driven by its appetite. We prayed that it would at least be able to recognize one of its own worshippers.

She would then need to wager with the violent violet Full flame. She would appeal to its craving for fuel and unconditional obedience. We were probably putting undue faith in Tabitha's persuasion skills when We devised this plan. Nevertheless, this was the case Tabitha had to artfully present: if the Full flame were to burn down the big house, then the flame would prove to the They that it could not be easily controlled. Tabitha would insist They were starting to believe the flame could be manipulated to meet their needs. The flame was meant to serve them and They were no longer obligated to serve the flame. This was certainly a direct affront to the flame's authority. This attitude demonstrated a defilement of its demanded and deserved praise.

By burning down the big house, the Full flame would assert its true power, magnitude, and hunger. This would compel the They to acknowledge the flame's might and to submit to its will. If the Full flame restrained itself and just burned down the house, it would probably provide the power necessary to build an even bigger furnace to house its burgeoning presence. The awestruck They would then be willing to build that new furnace for the Full flame. They really wouldn't have much of a choice to do otherwise, especially if They still wanted access to the flame's power.

In the end, the flame would receive more fuel, more praise, and more life from the They. And though the destruction of the big house would seem like a setback at first, the They, in turn, would become closer to their ultimate goal of having the flame live inside of them. If the flame agreed to these terms, it would allow Tabitha to use a stick to transfer a violet spark on to the big house's wooden floors. We would run into the forest as soon as We heard the crackling roar of the violet fire. Of course, Tabitha would then wake up her parents and the rest of the They to escape the house before it smoldered and crumbled into ashes. After a new big house was built, Tabitha could then reveal that she was the one behind the initial fire as a servant to the flame's will. Her parents would finally fully embrace her and the rest of the They would accept her as truly one of their own.

With this plan, if it all worked out, all parties involved would receive what they felt rightfully belonged to them. The flame would get its praise, the They would gain more Fullness, Tabitha would have a real family, and We would have our freedom.

* * *

Just a couple weeks later, as soon as We heard the crackling of wood coming from the big house, some of the They screamed and bolted out the front door. Tabitha had followed through for us. The diversion was in motion. This was our chance. This was for Isaac. This was for our future children. It was time to go.

We swiftly tiptoed out of our cabins into the forest. We refused to turn around, afraid of becoming pillars of salt, but We knew that Full flame continued to grow and ferociously devour the big house. We imagined that all They could do was watch with their mouths agape.

We glided through the woods until We knew We were out of earshot. Then We ran. We ran and ran and ran, feeling our collective pulse rush into our temples, our feet already bruised, splintered, and bloodied by sticks and stones on the ground. We were moving too quickly to feel the sting, knowing that if We were to stop, We would have keeled over in pain. And as We became a blur of motion with our eyes were fixed ahead, our minds could not help but wander back to the big farm. What could have really happened to the They?

Well, if the Full flame truly had restrained itself to just burning down the big house, then maybe They would follow through on the plan We outlined to Tabitha. They'd grow even closer to their goal. Perhaps They would continue on with the phases in the *Full* book, becoming more metallized as the flame became fully autonomous. Perhaps They really would remove their organs and the Full flame would be the greedy power that burned in the space in their chests where their hearts once were.

Perhaps They would get what They wanted. Oh, dear Lord. What a twisted tragedy of deception that would be.

But We quietly hoped that They would have a different fate. This was what We didn't tell Tabitha:

Perhaps the Full flame would be so greedy that it would not only destroy the big house, but it would also burn down the rest of the big farm. And then, its unabashed hunger might startle the They and inspire them to run, running as far away as possible from what They thought They wanted and needed. Perhaps They would run into the same wilderness where They first found us. They must have been just like us before the false hope of Fullness deceived them under the dark influence of the Embers. Maybe the distance from the violet flame would reverse the effects of its dark power. We hoped They would rediscover their humanity.

Maybe even They could be redeemed.

EPILOGUE

We have decided to walk a ways. Our limbs are aching but We move with a new resolve, wrapped in a gentle warmth. It is just past high noon but by some miracle, the sun is being kind as its rays blush through a soft lavender mist. We know that the days ahead are not always going to be like this. We know that We may face the greedy pain of hunger again. But We refuse to allow it to steal our humanity the way They greedily once tried. We choose to embrace the peace of this moment, a still part of our story. We are going toward the horizon. We know that the horizon is a place We may never reach in this life but We will always strive for it. We are far enough away now for the They to lose track of us. Maybe one day We'll even be far enough to truly pity them. Our wounds are too fresh right now, throbbing with resentment. But We do not want this. We want freedom. And We want to want the They to have freedom.

Even as We wrestle with our bitterness, We choose to pray for the They. Maybe these words will transform our hearts:

You all have wronged us,
but you have also been wronged.
You used us for our flesh
because you were told to hate your own,
counting it only as weakness.

You all have hurt us,
but still We pray for you.
We wish you the life and love
you've lost.

May you escape the deception
of the Embers' Fullness
and recognize your instilled worth.

We forgive you
because We know
God will make sure that justice is done.

May you all remember
your own humanity
and strive for your own horizon.

And though We can't resolve how We feel about her, We cannot help but imagine Tabitha's face as the prayer stirs in our souls. We still see the golden sheen of her skin, caught somewhere in the continuum between flesh and metal. When our hearts harden toward her, so does the image of her face. It becomes sharp, cold, and lifeless. But when our hearts soften, We see the face of a young woman with rosy cheeks who should have a better future. We see someone who *can* have a better future, even in the midst of the Great Famine. As long as They all make the right choice.

But who knows how long humanity can fall into the deceit of Fullness? Perhaps only God. Fullness, as the Embers orchestrated it, may reign during the Great Famine and beyond. They could not be alone in their weakness, people desperate to relinquish the vulnerability of their flesh. Full flames could exist in every seeable color, feasting on flesh and desire. Embers could be materializing from the Full flames' smoke. Darkness fueled by the fear of hunger and reverence of greed could choke the world.

Or maybe more of us, the We, could exist. May We know the power of the choice to become many in one, fleshed and all.

As for our beloved lost ones, though their bodies are somewhere among the Full flame's ashes, their souls are always with us. We'll carry their legacy in our bones and cherish them in our words, both in Common Tongue and our own language. We will remember Adelaide whenever We see an animal and try our best to respect it in all the ways We know how. We will see Rose when We take the time to watch a sunrise in all its golden glory. Our hearts will summon Samson every time We light a fire and tell stories around the benevolent, dancing flames. We will follow Zenith as We climb to new heights to experience and reflect on more of the world. We will imagine Jordan whenever cool blue waters envelop us as We swim.

And We will honor Isaac as We look into the wide, precious eyes of our future children. We know they will be as precocious as Adelaide but less naive. They will be warm-hearted like Rose but more trusting. Our children will be as strong as Samson and even more willingly vulnerable to those they love. They will be insightful like Zenith but less shy. They will be quick-witted like Jordan but less impulsive. And they will carry the hope We know We would have seen in Isaac's kaleidoscope eyes. We will make sure of that. We will make sure that our children feel loved and accepted as they navigate life in their flesh. We will help them discover what they like and don't like so they can begin to express their unique individuality. We will tell them it is okay to be sad and feel pain. Better to feel pain than to inflict it on others.

We will tell our children to beware of the Embers, for they may not always be figures in dark, hooded cloaks. Veiled in innocence, the Embers may try to appeal to the dark seed of greed in all of us. But for generations to come, We will know the evil of the Embers by their shape-shifting words.

We will walk together through our children's trials, supporting growth and healing as a community. We will tell our children that We will always be We.

And We will tell them, as long as We have breath in our lungs, that the ones who are fed are not always full.

THE THINGS WE CARRY

ADELAIDE'S FOREST-GREEN WOUND SALVE
- 3 scraped handfuls of besura moss (Or one handful if your hands are as large as Samson's.)
- 12 amtica flower petals
- 4 calympa leaves
- 1 slab of gerrylus bark
- 6 earthen bowls of rainwater
- 16 drops of jobtic tree sap
- 12 hefty sprinkles of deep green misla mup (It *cannot* be light green or brown.)

1. Use a large stone bowl and mortar to grind the besura moss, amtica flower petals, calympa leaves, and gerrylus bark together into a thick green paste.
2. Pour the rainwater, sprinkle the misla mud, and add the jobtic tree sap drops into a large metal pot and place it over a fire.
3. As the water and mud mixture starts to boil, slowly spoon in and stir the green paste. Continue stirring until the pot contents are a water-like consistency. Take the pot off the fire and place it in the shade to cool overnight.
4. By the morning, the pot mixture should have become a gel-like substance, which needs to be placed in small clay jars for storage. This recipe produces about eight jars total.

HOW ROSE CHOSE HER DAGGER

Every once and a while, as We watched Rose sharpen her beloved weapon against a makeshift whetstone, she'd notice she had an audience and begin to tell her dagger's origin story:

I come from a loving family. Though my parents were strict, they were gentle-hearted and would only be firm to protect us. My twin brother Rajon, well, if he had his way, would never even hurt a fly. He would only reluctantly kill the all too persistent cockroaches in our small apartment. Violence wasn't something anyone in my family believed in. We were all diplomats by nature, doing anything and everything to keep the peace. But we lived in a city where the air was always heavy with the whir of threats. Children were not allowed to leave their parents' sides in public. Violence, especially in its most covert forms, was the norm. Because of this, all the adult city inhabitants possessed some sort of weapon at all times. Traditionally, the men carried more obvious weapons. Probably some dramatic assertion of masculinity. My father had an axe that he made sure was polished and sharpened before strapping it around his waist each day. The women in turn carried the more discreet weapons. My mother kept a vial of poison that removed flesh upon contact in a specially lined pocket on the inside of her skirt. Rajon and I spent much of our childhood looking forward to the day we would have weapons of our own, which is quite sad now that I think about it.

When that day came, our parents took us to the city's best weapons shop. Rajon was immediately drawn to a golden bow with an impressive set of arrows. He thought it was beautiful and liked the idea of ensuring precision from a distance. Per the custom, I decided on something a bit simpler, something easier to hide. I chose this dagger because I also thought it was beautiful in a plainer way and I cared about a different type of precision. It seemed to me that anyone who would be a real threat would be someone who had managed to get too close.

SAMSON'S SONG (EXTENDED)

Verse One

How will the dawn come
now that you're gone?
How will the earth drink the morning dew?
How will my fire burn on
now that I don't have you?
You were the light I saw by.
You painted days golden hues.
And no matter where I was planted,
you were the reason why I grew.

Chorus

Though I may never be my full self again,
at least not the "me" you helped me become,
show me how to honor your memory
each time I rise before the sun.

Verse Two

Who will be my North Star
now that you're not here?
Who will remind the sky to wake up the moon?
Who will help me fight fear
now that darkness croaks its tune?
You showed me how to stand.
You placed your hand upon my heart.
And as I try to live without you
it's hard not to fall apart.

Chorus

Bridge

Why did the good Lord let you leave me?
I'll never know.
I just pray that soon
I'll hold you in my arms.
We'll find a place in the horizon
And you and I
will dwell together where the earth meets the sky.

Chorus

ZENITHISMS

- Survive to be alive and thrive.
- I'd really rather not, but I will because I care.
- No, Jordan. Just no. Love you, but no.
- Silence is only golden when you know everyone is free to speak.
- I love swimming and climbing. With swimming, I can face the depths, and with climbing, I can reach new heights.
- Oh my goodness. Just my, my, my goodness.
- You're carrying too much worry. Thank God it hasn't broken your back.
- I really wish that I knew how to make apple pie. I know if I could, it would make people smile.
- My life is a whirlwind in slow motion.
- You do realize that I just let you win, right?
- I keep my hair short so it's out of my way.
- Jordan, how many times are you going to make that joke and expect me to laugh?

HOW TO SWIM LIKE A JORDAN

First of all, before I bestow my wisdom upon you, you must know that you'll probably never swim as well as I do. I'm saving you from the otherwise inevitable disappointment. I've been swimming my whole life in all kinds of water for all kinds of reasons. So, I'm clearly a master. The only person to even come close to matching my ability is Zenith and her technique still has some flaws. But really, I'm glad that you want to learn how to swim like me and I'm more than happy to help. Here are a few tips to remember:

1. *Always enter the shallow part of the water feet first.* Diving into a body of water, especially one you're not familiar with, is never a good idea. Lord knows how deep it is or what's waiting at the bottom. I forgot this sage advice a couple of times and nearly hurt myself. I lucked out but don't take the risk.

2. *Don't waste your breath.* Gasping for air every time your head breaks through the water's surface will do you more harm than good. It'll drain your energy really quickly and make the whole experience more stressful. Trust that your body can fall into the rhythm of taking quick, full breaths at the end of every stroke or every other stroke, depending on your endurance.

3. *Be flexible with your stroke.* Different types of water call for different types of swimming, like different types of terrain call for different types of walking. Don't get me wrong. Technique is important but if you focus too much on perfecting your stroke, you might be making it harder for yourself. It doesn't take too long to find out which stroke you're most comfortable with in a given situation.

4. *Be mindful of currents but not afraid of them.* Water, like most things in life, is unpredictable. Sometimes currents

will catch you off guard. But if you panic about the currents before even getting in the water, then you'll never become a better swimmer. If you panic when you encounter an unexpected current while you're in the water, you won't be able to think clearly enough to ensure your safety.

5. *Don't imagine gazing into Zenith's eyes in the moonlight while you're swimming.* Believe me, I know it's tempting but I know this from experience. You'll lose focus and will literally be swept away.

TABITHA'S LETTER

Dear We People,

It took me a long time to gather the courage to write this letter. I would get in a lot of trouble if my parents found out I wrote it. You all would, too. They made me promise not to say anything about this to anyone and I don't like to break promises. So, I'm not going to say anything. I wrote all the important stuff instead. It's taking me a while to get to the real point. I'm so sorry but I am nervous about what you will think of everything when I finish explaining it. I'm worried about what you will think of me.

All of you are in danger and it's partially my fault. I have some confessions to make. You deserve to know as much of the truth as possible. I'll share everything I know.

After my father and his friends first brought you here, They assigned me the duty of watching over you while you ate. Not exactly to enforce the rule of eating every morsel. That was the rope tiers' responsibility. I was supposed to observe your behaviors and report my findings to my parents. They said if I did a good job, I would finally be approved to enter the next phase with everyone else. So, I tried to monitor you but by being around you so much, I really started to like your company. Proximity became affection, one could say. I cried a lot when Adelaide died. That wasn't supposed to happen. And I don't know if you know about this but I especially liked Jordan and I gave him a *Full* book so that he could become like me and the rest of my family. That really wasn't supposed to happen.

So then, my parents became concerned. They said They feared that my loyalty to their cause had been compromised. To prove I was faithful, my family said I had to hurt one of you. I didn't want to do it. Please know that. But if I didn't do it, my parents said They would disown me. So, I put a small amount of poison inside of Rose's cream puff. I thought it would only make her sick for a couple of days. But my family, knowing my weakness for you all, must have guessed my plan and put a more concentrated solution of the poison in the vial. And when Rose died, I swear a part of me died with her. Honest. Afterward, my parents fully accepted me and my legs didn't have to be tied to the chairs anymore. But still, I will never forgive myself for what I've done. Ever.

I know you must hate me now. I would hate me now too if I were you. But I want to somehow do something to show you I am not like my family. I wish I could be more like you. Losing Adelaide, Rose, Samson, Zenith, and Jordan, especially Jordan, was absolutely devastating. Watching my family feed all their dead bodies to the Full furnace flame broke my heart, especially after finding out Zenith was pregnant. But to move into the next phase with my family, my heart isn't allowed to be breakable. Soon, I won't even have a heart to break.

A lot of what I've written probably doesn't make any sense but it will soon. Please read the *Full* book I gave to Jordan. You'll have to do it secretly or you'll get in trouble. Please. You all need to trust me on this. I know I don't deserve it but please. Trust me.

Sincerely,

Tabitha

PS. You are part of Phase Three. At least that's what I've heard my parents say.

PPS. My parents have also said They got the *Full* books from a wise figure wearing a dark, hooded cloak. I'm not sure what that means or if that's important but I mentioned that I'd share everything I know. Now I have.

ZENITH AND JORDAN'S LIST OF POTENTIAL BABY NAMES

GIRLS

~~Amber~~

Azara

~~Esther~~

~~Jasmine~~

Zephyra

~~Demitrea~~

~~Estelle~~

Angel

Naomi

~~Shoshana~~

BOYS

~~Matthias~~

~~Alexander~~

~~Jonathan~~

Isaac

Levi

Kaleb

Titus

Josiah

Micah

Christian

FIRST PAGE OF THE *FULL* BOOK

Full: Your New Furnace and the Flame Beyond Humanity

Table of Contents

May Fullness burn within you all.

ACKNOWLEDGMENTS

The We and the They would have never come into fruition if it weren't for the "Wes" that have shaped this story and me for the better. I would be remiss not to take the opportunity to first and foremost thank my family:

Mark Dawkins, Ingrid Powell Dawkins, Kendra Dawkins, Kori Dawkins, Mason Dawkins, Marilyn Dawkins, Tashirah Powell, Steven Powell, Michael Knight, William Kelley, and the rest of my incredible relatives.

I'd also like to gratefully acknowledge my wonderful beta readers, who have become like family to me through the years and through this book journey:

Albert Ratner, Paul Yu, Daniel P. Farina, Jessica Silver Leonard, Gaylord W. Greene, Hope Owens, Cheryl Huguley, Serena Michaels, Trisha Campbell, Shalela Dowdy, Exter G. Gilmore III, Eric Koester, Judy Rosman, Julia Jackson, Keith E. Brown, Natalie Mandry, Amy Conforte, G. W. Yeager, Celia Krefter, Tosin Sanusi, Elijah Schultz, Kelly DeLuca, Kyra Citron, Shandrea Patton, Angela M. Holmes, Perry Edgerton Thomas, Robert Alfred Willard, Sean Kim, Sean Jordan, Mara Measor, Nathan Rubene dos Santos, Brandon Shi, Zoe Chan, Melanie Duenas, Nicky Don, Tracy Simmons, Tobie Lane, John Tran, Alexandria Beightol, Michele Bourne, John Stark, Dr. Isabelle Zaugg, Sara Mead, Sophie Byrne, Mo-man Yu, Simon To, William To, Alex To, Ava Ligh, Kayla Schiffer, Shalom Omollo, Amanda Friery, Laura Isham, Sheila Wright, Cody Kanz, Mel Choi, Kai Tinsley, Angela Song, Jade Moses, Tammy Kay Barry, Anthony Argenziano, and Amaya Howard-Carswell.

I can never adequately express my appreciation for all of your support.

Lastly, I'd like to thank you, dear reader, for becoming a "We" with me through this story. Thank God this is not the end.

Made in the USA
Columbia, SC
13 August 2020